Christmas with the Firefighter

Christmas with the Firefighter

A Cape Hope Romance

Clare Connelly

TULE
PUBLISHING

Christmas with the Firefighter

Tule Publishing First Printing, August 2019

The Tule Publishing, Inc.

First Publication by Tule Publishing 2019

Cover design by Hang

ISBN: 978-1-951190-18-7

Prologue

Christmas, twenty years ago.

"STOP YELLING!" THE whispered words fell from Ally's lips as she held her slender frame hard against the door of her room.

The incantation didn't help.

Their voices exploded through the house, first her mother's—a shriek, just like when Molly's paw had gotten caught under the car tire. It had been the most awful noise Ally had ever heard, and her mother's voice was like it now, rent with pain, bordering on hysterical.

Then came her father's—slurred and angry, loud, aggressive. Ally huddled, her knees to her chest, wrapping her arms around them and burying herself as best she could within her own fragile embrace.

She murmured "stop yelling" over and over, a prayer she hoped would be answered.

Their words weren't discernible, but the fighting dragged. Every time there was a lull, she lifted her head a little, only for it to begin again a moment later. There was the slamming of a door, then more yelling. The breaking of glass. She squeezed her eyes shut, her heart hammering against her ribs, her face paler than the snow that was drifting down outside the window.

Ally stayed where she was, rocking against the door, her bedroom freezing—they'd forgotten to turn the heat on, they'd seemingly forgotten she existed, which happened when they fought—and she waited.

She waited until her mother's fury morphed into tears and, eventually, there was silence. The kind of silence six-year-old Ally knew would bleed into the next day, as her parents used silence to continue their fight.

Her eyes lifted to the other wall—she'd made a nativity scene in class, and she scrambled across the floor and pulled the baby Jesus from its center, cuddling it in the palm of her hand and hoping it would add weight to her incantation.

Ally crawled into bed, holding Jesus, telling herself it would be okay. That the morning would clear out the night, the fight would pass, and everything would be fine.

It wasn't fine.

Sometime between the awful, hours-long argument and the new day's break, in the middle of the night, when the snow was falling thickest, Jack Monroe grabbed his jacket and car keys and left home, apparently without a backward glance.

It would be twenty years before Ally saw him again—and she suspected she'd never be able to forgive him.

Chapter One

IT WAS A saving grace for Stella that she was so much like her mom when she was cross. Whenever Luke Miller felt his patience wearing thin at yet *another* temper tantrum, he'd look at his six-year-old daughter and see Jen—wavy blond hair, huge green eyes, a nose that lifted at its tip—and his anger would dissipate, just like that.

Okay, not quite "just like that," and it didn't completely disappear, but it took the edge off a little, just enough for him to remember that he was the adult, and Stella the kid, and the fact he felt like screaming or throwing something was a childish impulse he definitely shouldn't indulge.

"Just have a few bites," he cajoled.

Stella made no effort to pick up her fork. "I. Don't. Like. It."

Luke didn't visibly react even as his temper ratcheted up a couple of notches. "You did a week ago."

"No. I. Didn't."

He lifted his own fork to his mouth, shoveling some of the pasta in. It wasn't great. He'd followed the recipe—at least, he thought he had—but it hadn't turned out anything like the picture. Still, it was food—edible as a baseline, and damn it, he was getting fed up with Stella's bursts of attitude. "It's tomatoes, onion, basil, cheese. Nothing suspicious there. See?" He lifted another scoop to his mouth, his eyes hooked to Stella's the whole time.

Her lower lip pouted belligerently, and again he thought of Jen. Not because of their physical similarities but because of Jen's ability to cope, to smile, to know how to handle just about everything.

Jen would have known what to do. Jen would have a joke or a story, a promise, something that would have worked.

Or maybe she would have taken Stella's side and insisted the pasta really was a complete flop, and she'd have laughed at him for his lack of culinary skills and suggested they go down the street to Tucker's and grab burgers instead. This close to Christmas, she'd have probably made them sing carols the whole way—Jen had loved Christmas in a way Luke had always teased her for but found himself longing for every year now.

It had been over six years since Jen had passed, and he didn't grieve for her in the same way now as he had then. The stick of dynamite that had blown into his life the night she'd died, spreading everything into disarray, was more of a slow burn these days.

Memory was a funny beast, intangible, yet ever present. He'd be walking down Main Street, and he'd see her in his mind as clear as anything—library books in hand, a grin on her face, those beautiful floral dresses she'd seemed to have an endless supply of. He'd later discovered she made them out of thrift shop fabrics. The way she'd smelled like violets and summer all year round. The way she'd cried when he'd enlisted, begging him not to go away again. The way she'd cried—different tears this time—when he'd proposed.

The words she'd used when she'd written him and told him about the baby.

His gut clenched at that particular memory—how in the desert of Iraq, among the tents of Camp Freedom, he'd learned that he was going to be a dad, and all the dust and the dirt and the heat and the sweat, the death and the certainty that you would be next had paused, everything had fallen silent, and for a second he'd been back in Cape Hope, under the shade of the huge Sycamore tree they'd loved forever, Jen's head against his chest, her heart beating with his.

Jen's ghost was everywhere, and he was grateful for that. Grateful she was still somehow alive in this town, and so much of her was in the daughter she'd died bringing into the world.

Stella pushed her plate away and sat back in her chair.

This part of their daughter, though, was all him. Stubborn as a mule, she'd go to bed hungry before she'd admit defeat and try the pasta.

He had another mouthful, his temper rising. "You know

what, Stella? If you don't want it, that's fine. Go have a bath."

She opened her mouth to say something and then snapped it shut. "Whatever." She scraped her chair back in a way he was darned sure was intentionally noisy, shot him a filthy look, then turned around and stomped from the room.

He sat there a moment, staring at her empty chair.

Silence filled the old house.

And it *was* old, the plumbing mostly left over from when the place had been built at the turn of the last century. It sang every time it was pushed into service, just for a moment or two.

And it wasn't singing now. Whatever Stella was doing, it wasn't what she'd been told.

Expelling a breath, he stood up, moving out of the big old kitchen and down the hallway.

He found his daughter sitting on the floor of her room, her shirt off but still in her jeans and shoes, playing with the doll's house. If she hadn't already goaded him senseless this afternoon, he might have laughed. She was so easily distracted—like a goldfish, he often thought, wishing Jen were here to laugh about it with him. Wishing there was someone to laugh about it with, to smile lovingly at this beautiful, complex, exhausting little girl.

"Stella Jennifer Miller. Bath. Now."

She lifted her face to his, something like hurt in her eyes, and his gut churned. He propped his hip against the doorjamb and rolled his head on his neck for a minute. It had been a long day; he was tired. He wanted Stella in bed so he could crack a beer and sit out on the deck a moment, staring at the fields and the stars and not thinking of anything. "I'm tired."

"Yeah, so am I. So have your bath and you can go to bed."

"Can't I just skip it tonight?"

He pulled a face. "You've been playing down by the creek with the Watkins kids, right? Do you really want to get in your sheets with leeches and gunk all over you?"

A smile tickled the corner of her lips, but she swallowed it, glaring at him determinedly. "I don't have leeches."

"How do you know? They could be behind your knees. You know they love it there."

"I didn't get wet, Daddy. It's, like, minus a hundred today."

He shifted his gaze to the window. It was already dark out, but with just a tiny lick of purple still lighting the sky. "It's not that bad. Bath. Come on."

"Fine," she huffed, and he knew that it was the thought of leeches that had done it.

He watched her disappear down the corridor, into the bathroom, and a minute later the water started to run, and the ancient pipes burst into a grudging baritone. He moved back to the kitchen, picked up their dinner bowls, and carried them to the garbage can.

He'd make a sandwich for himself later.

He stacked the plates in the sink and braced his palms on the counter, staring out at the darkness beyond the kitchen window, breathing in, breathing out, trying to calm down, trying not to take any of Stella's mood personally.

Stella's teacher was always full of praise for the little girl. *She's one of the sweet ones, Luke. Try not to worry so much.* But he did worry.

He worried all the time.

He worried that Stella was growing up and away from him, that the smiling little girl she'd been even a year ago was morphing into some kind of adolescent already. And it was too early, wasn't it? It seemed way too early, but how the heck did he know?

He had no experience; he was flying blind. He'd been doing okay for a long time. The baby years had been tough, but tough in a way he was kind of weirdly used to. Two tours in Iraq and his training in the Marines had prepared him for mental and physical exhaustion, as had his call-outs here in Cape Hope as a volunteer firefighter. He hadn't minded the sleepless nights and the erratic hours Stella had kept to.

Toddlerhood hadn't exactly been a walk in the park, but he'd muddled his way through—learning more than he thought possible about My Little Pony.

But this was something else. He was living with a first-grader tyrant.

The water cut off, and he moved to the ancient fridge, pulled out a beer, unscrewed the top, and slung the lid in the garbage, all the while listening for Stella's splishing and splashing. Soon after, the sound of the water draining filled the house.

He stayed where he was, butt pressed against the countertop. Stella appeared a moment later, her skin pink from the bath, her pajamas fluffy, with unicorns all over them.

"You done?" He leaned forward, ruffling her shiny blond hair.

She nodded, standing still, looking up at him with Jen's eyes, and his gut tightened. "Yep."

"Right. Bed for you, butterfly."

A smile flickered at the corners of her lips and all of the frustration over dinners not eaten washed away. He wished she'd smile more. "I'm not tired anymore."

"You were a minute ago."

She lifted her shoulders. "I'm not now."

"Then you can read a bit. Come on." He lifted her up then, wondering how much longer he'd be able to do that for before she started complaining about it as well. He carried her into her room and deposited her beside the bed. "You've got your library book?"

She nodded. "But it's boring."

"Seriously?"

She nodded once more, more emphatically. "Yes, Daddy. Seriously."

"So take it and exchange it tomorrow. Get a better one."

She bit down on her lip, like she was going to say something but didn't want to. He hovered by the door, waiting.

"Stella? Tomorrow?"

She expelled a dramatic sigh. "Yeah, sure."

He watched as she climbed into bed, grabbing her book off the nightstand and pulling out the bookmark she'd made from a feather and some cardboard.

"'Night, Daddy."

His heart stuttered. "'Night, baby."

She fixed him with a cool gaze over the top of her book. "I'm not a baby."

Luke let out a short laugh. "No, you're definitely not. Lights out in twenty minutes."

❦

IT WAS A frosty night—not quite as arctic as Stella had suggested, but cool enough that when Luke stepped out onto the porch and took a seat on the wide, wooden steps, beer in one hand, eyes trained on the outline of the sycamore tree by the drive, his breath emerged like a cloud from inside him.

It was just under a month until Christmas. Winter was firmly upon them, wrapping around all of North Carolina, blowing ice in off the Atlantic, shrouding the trees in mist and wind, bracing everything with a coldness that should have been bleak, but which was, instead, breathtaking and beautiful.

The air was different here in Cape Hope.

Clean and bracing all at once.

Even in summer when the sun baked the earth and the flowers grew wild, covering all the farms and fields in color and the fragrance of burnt honey, there was still something refreshing about this place.

Perhaps it was the elemental beauty of it? The sound of the ocean rolling against the other side of town, the creek that ran through the back parts, the green that grew wild over every lawn and rolling hill.

Or maybe it was being back here, when he'd wondered if he would ever see these fields and faces again.

War was a funny thing. You didn't do a tour meaning to think about death, but one way or another, its inevitability hit you in the face—so it became something you expected, something you braced for.

He'd braced for it. That last tour had been rough. So many times he'd thought his number was up. And he'd thought about Jen, and the baby in her belly, and somehow he'd made it through.

Not in a million years had it occurred to him that it would be Jen who didn't make it. That it would be Jen, who, here, in the safety and beauty of this little town time forgot, in a place like a hospital, with doctors and nurses and equipment, would suddenly cease to exist.

He'd gotten used to losing friends—he'd gotten used to

empty tents, stretchers, depleted units. He'd gotten used to seeing multiple dog tags around the guys' necks. Absent-mindedly, he lifted his hands to his throat and pulled his own out, feeling the ridges of his tag and that of his buddy Wade, who'd been shot by a sniper two days after he'd gotten to Baghdad, on his third tour.

He knew about death.

He'd walked among it. He'd flirted with it. Hell, he'd practically invited it a few times.

But losing Jen hadn't been anywhere on his radar. Not once did he imagine anything would happen to her.

She'd been *here*, so far from war and guns and tanks and the steady march of death. But wars weren't limited to battlefields, and her body had taken against her, in such a way that no doctor could save her.

All they could do was cut Stella from Jen's body, passing the little baby over to Luke. He'd held his pink, breathing, screaming daughter as he'd stared down at the wife who had left him, the woman he'd loved since they were kids in kindergarten and he'd let her share his lunch.

He threw back his beer, cradling the bottom of the glass bottle, his eyes lifting to the stars overhead. So familiar to him he could lie down and close his eyes and trace the sky by memory.

In the beginning, when Jen had died, he'd been inundated with help. That's the way it went in tight-knit communities. Over the years, the help had decreased. He wasn't a grieving husband, newly widowed, dealing with a newborn infant anymore. Things got easier.

Didn't they?

He frowned, unconsciously looking over his shoulder toward the house.

Stella wasn't easy right now. He couldn't remember the last time they'd gone through a day without butting heads. When she was in a foul mood, she was a lost cause.

But when she was happy? She was just the sweetest little thing on earth.

She's tired, you know? First grade's a big step up from kindergarten. New friends, new skills. She's just having a bumpy landing.

Luke prayed Stella's teacher knew what she was talking about—and that they'd find smooth ground again soon.

HER SCREAMS WOKE him.

He'd been in a deep sleep, his own dreamless. He pushed out of bed, striding down the hallway and into Stella's room. She was sobbing, her bunny cuddled to her chest. He felt his way to her nightstand and flicked on the lamp. "It's okay, baby, it's okay."

There was no protest about the nickname now. She grabbed at his chest, scrambling up to sit in his lap, and she stayed huddled there a moment, her sobs softer but still racking her little body.

"It's okay," he murmured against her fine hair, stroking it gently. "It's just a bad dream."

She nodded again, hugging close to him. He held her until her crying calmed and her breathing slowed, and then he eased her back down onto her pillow. "Daddy?"

He paused, standing by the bed. "Yeah?"

"Can you leave the light on?"

His heart turned over for his little girl. "Yeah, Stella. I'll leave the light on." He understood how light in the dark helped; he understood how it could take away nightmares, frighten away evil. He pressed a kiss against her forehead, and she smiled sweetly.

"It's the fair tomorrow."

He looked at the watch he wore on his wrist—a gift from his grandpa when he signed up to the Marines. Not everyone had hated the idea as much as Jen had. "Later today, actually. All the more reason for you to shut your eyes and get some Zs."

Chapter Two

Ally Monroe had decided to use a fake name somewhere on the road between Indiana and Kentucky, as she'd made the drive east from Wisconsin with this sleepy little place in mind. It had seemed sensible. The last thing she wanted was for her father to know she was in town before she was ready to confront him.

If he was even still here.

This place was just exactly what Ally would have imagined if she'd ever put her mind to conjuring up an image of a small-town diner. Linoleum floors, booths on either side of the room that looked like they hadn't been changed since the fifties, a low roof strung now with tinsel and fairy lights in honor of the Christmas season, and a cake counter brimming with good, honest country fare. Muffins and carrot cake and slices of pie as big as Ally's hands. She shot a glance at the counter, tempted by the food even though she'd eaten only an hour or so out of town. Food wasn't simply practical for chefs, though, and Ally was a passionate chef, and lover of flavor.

"You on your way to the fair?" The woman at the cash

register smiled.

Ally looked toward the diner's windows, to the main street of Cape Hope, a town about an hour out of Wilmington. Christmas hadn't been confined to the diner; lights were strung from one side of the wide boulevard-style street to the other, glowing warm in contrast to the wintry hue of the trees that were spindly and gnarled behind the old buildings. "The fair?"

"The Christmas Fair," the woman elaborated, her surprise evident that perhaps Ally hadn't heard of it. "Craft, mulled wine, a bonfire—out on the Heyworth Estate. Worth a look, even if you're just passing through."

"Sounds fun." And it did, but a Christmas fair wasn't the reason she'd come to town. She was in Cape Hope for one reason and one reason only. The envelope she'd found behind her mother's bed when she'd been cleaning out the house sat folded neatly in her handbag, the postmark burned into her brain. CAPE HOPE, NC.

It was strange how, so many years after he'd left, a small detail such as his handwriting could evoke such a visceral emotional response. But twenty-six-year-old Ally had found the envelope from where it had no doubt been long forgotten by life and time, and had seen Jack Monroe's scratchy scrawl—and her heart had tripped.

Her dad.

The little notes from around the house—shopping lists, inscriptions in books, the letter he'd written Ally on her first day of school that she'd ripped up when he'd left home—and taped back together the next day.

"I'm actually looking for someone."

"Well, whoever it is, chances are they'll be at the bonfire. Not many people in this neck of the woods who miss it." The older woman looked pointedly at the clock above the door, making it clear she was impatient to close up.

Ally smiled apologetically. "Right. Just the coffee then, thanks. To go." She placed some coins on the counter and took the drink. "You don't happen to know Jack Monroe, do you?" She pushed the words out casually enough, but her voice was squeaky to her own ears.

Saying his name aloud did something funny to Ally's insides, as though a whole kaleidoscope of butterflies had begun to bounce around. Her mom had forbidden her to talk about him, and that was a habit Ally had stuck to for a long time. All this time, all this way, and by saying his name aloud it was almost as though she might be able to conjure him out of thin air.

"What's he look like?"

Doubt made her stomach swoop. Because she had no idea. The man was her father, and all she had was a twenty-year-old memory. "Tall, slim," she said thoughtfully, describing him as he'd been then. "Blue eyes."

The woman shook her head. "Sorry, darlin'. Don't know anyone by that name and I know most people 'round these parts. Go see Andy Heyworth out at the fair—he might be able to help you."

Ally nodded, telling herself not to lose heart. It was way too early for that.

"Andy knows everyone and everything," the woman continued. "And if Jack Monroe lives in Cape Hope, he's bound to be there himself."

Ally's heart lurched at the thought of that, anticipation at war with uncertainty and dread. "Thanks."

"Don't mention it." The woman was already flicking off the lights for the display cases on the counter.

Ally sipped the coffee, shouldering her way out of the diner right as a man approached. He quickstepped to grab the handle and hold it open for her, and the little girl at his side with straw-blond hair and a ready smile looked up at Ally.

"Hey," the girl said.

Ally smiled back. "Hi yourself."

"You going to the fair?"

Ally lifted her brows. "I'm not sure." Her gaze pulled upward, to the man who was presumably the girl's father. He was—by any measuring stick—handsome. Tall and strong, he looked like he lived and breathed country air. His tan was golden, his hair dark and close-cropped, his eyes a dark brown flecked with caramel. He had a square jaw and strong features that added to the impression of a sort of latent power.

"Everyone's going to the fair," the little girl persisted.

"Okay, Stella," the man spoke, his voice thick and graveled—perfect for him—a smile tilting his lips. "The lady might have somewhere else she's got to be. Leave her alone."

"No, it's fine. I'm…I thought I might head that way. Check it out." Her expression showed nonchalance as she dug her spare hand into the pocket of her jeans.

"Oh, you gotta," the little girl rushed. "It's so much fun. There's dancing and rides and chestnuts, and everyone goes."

Ally's smile was spontaneous. "Well, if there's chestnuts." She winked.

The little girl nodded. "And cotton candy."

Ally laughed. "Is it pink?"

"Yep."

"Then how can I miss it?"

The girl looked up at her dad, her look one of total childish adoration. "Daddy says grown-ups don't like cotton candy."

Ally shot a look of apology toward the man. "I think I'm not a very good grown-up."

"You look like one."

"Oookay, Stella," he interrupted, but his grin showed just the same adoration for his daughter as she felt for him. Ally's heart did a funny little jerk, long-ago memories of feeling just that same kind of love and affection for her dad swarming through her. "Let's get in here before the diner closes."

Stella put her hand in her dad's. "Okay. But you go to

the fair."

Ally bit back a grin. "I will." She directed her attention to the man, her heart kicking for a whole other reason now. "The lady said it's that way?" She pointed with her coffee cup down the road.

"Yeah, head about a mile down the road, then take the left turn. You can't miss it—giant Christmas tree sign."

"We helped paint it," Stella said proudly.

"That we did." The man grinned, his teeth white, a dimple deepening in one stubbled cheek.

Ally didn't know what was wrong with her—she'd seen more than her fair share of handsome men, but there was something about this guy that had her heart scuttling against her ribs. She flicked her gaze downward, feeling a lot more comfortable talking to the little girl. "I'll keep an eye out for it then." But, in spite of herself, Ally's attention was drawn back to the man's face.

"We might see you there." He grinned and her stomach formed knots.

"Maybe." Noncommittal. Perfect. She wasn't in Cape Hope to make friends, even really handsome ones with sweet, friendly daughters. Friends would complicate things. The whole point of coming here, armed with a fake name, was so she could fly under the radar until she was ready to confront Jack Monroe.

Having your heart broken by your dad once was bad enough. She was pretty sure she didn't want to repeat the performance. She had to control this at every step—no way would she risk him learning of her whereabouts before she wanted him to.

There was no guarantee he would even be here anymore. When she thought about it, which she'd done a lot on the drive from Wisconsin, it was pretty flimsy.

An envelope that was years old, obviously long forgotten by her mom.

It was possible he'd just been passing through town when he'd mailed it, that whatever he'd sent had been done from the road, on his way to somewhere else, or maybe even while on vacation. Then again, Cape Hope was a bit quiet to be on the tourist map. Wasn't it just as likely he'd lived here? Maybe still did?

"Well"—she nodded, a crisp shift of her head that made her ponytail bob—"I might see you later."

"We'll be eating all the cotton candy," Stella promised with a mischievous grin.

"You'll be having a little cotton candy," the father said, lifting his hand in farewell as he ushered Stella into the diner. "And only if you have something healthy first. You've got too much of a sweet tooth, just like your mom."

The rest of the words trailed into nothingness as the door shut behind them.

It was a brusque winter evening, ice in the air, so Ally held a hand out, trying to catch a tiny little speck, wishing it would turn to snow.

It felt cold enough, anyway. With a last, longing look at the sky, she unlocked her Prius, slipping behind the wheel. Another sip of coffee before she turned the engine over and gave one last look toward the diner, just in time to see the woman inside sliding a chocolate mint to the girl while her dad's back was turned.

Ally pulled out from the curb, still smiling, the lingering hint of the man's cologne teasing her nostrils the whole way to the fair.

As it turned out, she hadn't really needed directions after all. About half a mile away from the main street, cars had pulled over, lined up on both sides of the road, and as she turned left, she saw the glowing warmth of a bonfire and strings of lights strung overhead between trees. Music blared, so that, even in her car, she could hear the solid country beat.

A young guy in a reflective jacket pointed his thumb behind him. She wound down her window and slowed the car to a crawl. "More parking in the fallow field." He nodded to his right. "Take what you can."

Ally nodded, pulling through a big white farm gate and finding a spot near the fence. She stepped out of the car, grabbing her coffee and locking the doors, looking around with a faster-rushing heart.

In the next field over she could see hundreds of people celebrating; the smell of pumpkin and spice filled the air and, like a moth to a flame, she moved forward, tugged by some kind of invisible thread, until she was among the crowd.

Was it possible that Jack Monroe was here?

A man in his fifties sauntered past, and hope burst inside Ally.

Why not? Why couldn't that be possible?

Going further, she pretended interest in a table set up to sell jewelry, then moved on to a stand with roasted chestnuts, to another with spiced cider, until she came upon kids dipping apples in toffee with great care.

Memories of her own childhood slammed against her—her mom had loved this time of year. Halloween, Thanksgiving, Christmas—she'd marked each occasion with zealous enthusiasm, decorating their house, knitting Christmas sweaters each year, making pomanders with Ally until the whole house had smelled like orange and cloves.

Longing tore through Ally for a moment, and she stopped walking, taking a last sip from her coffee, then cradling the empty paper cup. She stared straight ahead, seeing nothing, her heart cracking into a billion pieces.

It had all been so sudden. She'd spoken to her mom earlier that day and then suddenly she was gone.

It had been six months, and it hadn't got any easier. Some days, she thought things were getting better. Then there was fall, and Halloween, and no mom to decorate the house with. Thanksgiving had been the last straw. Ally had never felt so lonely as she had bringing a meager turkey wing and leftover pumpkin pie home from the restaurant for her solitary dinner.

Ally swallowed past the familiar feeling of tears clawing at her throat and looked around the fair. It was like trying to find a needle in a haystack, but she had to start somewhere. She'd driven all this way after months of thinking about it, building up her courage, deciding she couldn't live the rest of her life not knowing.

Her dad had run out on her, on both of them, and for years Ally had smothered her hurt in anger, telling herself she hated him. And a part of her did, even though he was her dad.

But he was also the only family she had left. She couldn't live the rest of her life without at least knowing something about him—and without knowing *why* he'd abandoned her.

"Free tickets to the Ferris wheel." A man walked past, holding out a little book of tickets. "Ma'am?"

Ally shook her head, waving him off with a tight smile, moving away, deeper into the crowd and closer to the source of the music. A stage had been set up in front of a barn and a makeshift dance floor laid in the field. It was packed, the dancing happy, fast, confident—Christmas songs given an up-tempo beat that rang out through the field. Ally stood on the edges, watching, frowning.

Because it had seemed kind of simple when she'd set out for Cape Hope, but now that she was here, she had no real clue where to start—especially since she didn't want to give away her true connection to Jack Monroe until she knew more about his life. She'd thought about that a lot over the years. How she'd feel if she ever saw him again. What she'd say. And like most things you speculated about ahead of time, Ally was smart enough to know it would only be in the actual moment that she could say with any real certainty how she'd respond.

"You wanna dance, ma'am?" a deep voice came from behind Ally.

She looked around, a polite smile on her lips. Did this place breed tall, dark, and handsome or what? "I'm not really much of a dancer."

"The music makes *everyone* a dancer." His grin was pure charm. "Wanna see?" He put a hand on his belt buckle and moved his feet.

A smile lifted the corners of her lips. "Impressive." She turned her attention back to the crowd. "But I'm pretty sure, no matter how good the music is, I'm a lost cause."

His grin grew wider. "Fair enough. A drink then?"

She eyed him thoughtfully. "I'm actually looking for someone."

"A date?"

"No. Not exactly." Not even a little bit; she wasn't sure why she'd said that. She shook her head to blow the words away.

"Want a hand?"

"Finding him?" she prompted, tilting her head to the side as she considered this. "Yeah, maybe. Have you ever met a guy called Jack Monroe?"

The man thought about it for a moment, considering the question, then shook his head. "Nah, can't say I have. Where's he live?"

"I thought around here." She grimaced. "At least, he used to. It's been a while—we lost touch. I was hoping he was still in town."

"A relative of yours?"

"No." The lie felt weird; she'd never been good at lies, even little ones. But she had to do this. Confronting the man who ran out on you twenty years ago wasn't something you did casually. She wanted to hold all the cards if and when she found Jack Monroe. Reassured by the necessity of this small fib, she pushed on. "He's just someone my mom used to know."

"Sorry I can't help you..." He let the words trail off like he was waiting for her to answer.

"Amy." She used the fake name she'd decided on halfway here—in for a penny, in for a pound. "Amy James." And despite the fact she felt the necessity of this, being untruthful still sat heavily in her gut.

"Pleasure to meet you, Amy James. I'm Mattias Diaz—everyone calls me Matt." He led her through the crowds toward the drinks stand, where he ordered a couple of ciders. "If he was in town, someone here'll know him. Cape Hope's like that—kind of a living memory, hard to hide anything in these parts."

"Yeah?"

"You're not from here?"

"No." She wrinkled her nose. "I'm just here looking for…Jack." There was a slight pause as she almost said "my dad." She smiled to cover it. "The lady at the diner—"

"Katie," he supplied.

"Right, Katie." She remembered that being on her name badge now. "She said maybe a guy called Andy Heyworth might be able to help?"

"Yeah, could be." Matt turned around so his back was to the bar, propping his elbows on the top, the picture of relaxation. "You'll have to wait a bit, though. He's run off his feet with the fair."

Impatience zipped through Ally. She hid it. "It's his place?"

"Yeah."

"And he does this every year?"

"Been going on since he was a kid." Matt confirmed with a nod, sliding his eyes sideward to meet Ally's. "Only missed one year—nineteen forty-three, on account of the war and most of the town's men being away. Wasn't much to celebrate."

"No, I guess not." She sipped her cider; it was delicious. So much so she took another sip again quickly and imagined how well it would go with pork and slaw, all sticky and sweet.

"So you're going to be around awhile?"

Ally shrugged. "Depends on if I find Jack."

"Then I'd better help you find him." Matt wiggled his brows flirtatiously, and Ally returned his smile with one of her own, but she found herself thinking back to the man outside the diner, her eyes scanning the crowd looking for his face without even realizing it.

Matt, though, wasn't easy to shake, and she had to admit, his company was pleasant. She liked chatting with him, and he sure was a fount of wisdom. If she'd been writing a paper on the town's history, he'd have been an excellent research source.

As they moved through the fair, going from the bar, past the dance floor, to the holly and ivy vines that had been shaped into enormous wreaths and were lit with little candles, Ally found herself genuinely captivated by his recounting of town history. From the stories of hauntings down by the water to the art deco theater that the town had raised funds to build back in the twenties by selling pots of jam right up the east coast, Cape Hope was quickly becoming some kind of storybook place in Ally's mind.

Had it been like this for her dad?

Had he found his way here and decided it was too quaint, too sweet, to even think of leaving? Was he at this very fair somewhere, drinking cider, wandering around, dancing? Living his life with no recollection, no care, for the girl he'd once claimed to love and had walked away from as though she meant nothing? Hurt simmered in her chest, but it was a hurt she knew well, a hurt she was adept at folding away for later.

"Andy'll be over by the wheel. He likes to keep an eye on it and make sure it doesn't topple," Matt said with an affectionate roll of his eyes. "No matter how many engineers tell him it's safe as houses, he likes to be there himself. As though he could do anything if it did fall."

Ally smiled at the picture that painted. "How long does the fair run?"

"Just one night." He lifted his broad shoulders. "Kind of a lot of trouble to go to for one night, I know, but we all love it."

"I can see why," she said simply, surprised that it was true. She'd always thought this sort of thing was kitschy, but standing in the midst of the Christmas Fair, the spirit of the season wrapped around her, for a second she could almost forget how alone she was, and how darned much she missed her mom.

"Yeah. We all do." He winked and nodded to their right, so Ally took a step that way before colliding with something hard and firm, like a wall, except warm and mobile.

A hand snaked out to steady her, and there was an apology offered, soft and in that Southern drawl that sent goosebumps running over her skin. His hand on her forearm darted little arrows through her blood. Ally looked up and met the eyes of the man from the diner.

"Hey, it's you." His apology morphed into a grin, all white teeth and stubbled jaw, dimpled cheek and sparkling eyes.

"It's me." Ally rubbed her shoulder, which was vibrating a little from the force of his knock.

"You know each other?" Matt asked, not able to hide the disappointment in his voice.

"We met at the diner," Ally explained.

"We didn't technically meet," the man corrected. "I didn't catch your name, anyway."

Matt waved a hand toward Ally. "Amy James, this is Luke Miller."

"Pleasure to meet you, Amy. You made quite an impression on Stella; she's been scouting for you since we arrived."

"We were just over that way." She hitched a thumb across the fair.

"I was trying to convince her to give the dance floor a go." Matt grinned.

"And you should be grateful I refused."

"We're heading to the Ferris wheel now," Matt offered by way of a departure.

Only Luke shrugged, turning around. "I'll come with you. Stella's with Jacob, no doubt conning him into more treats."

"That's an uncle's prerogative, right?" Matt pointed out.

Ally smiled. "She's very sweet. How old is she?"

They walked side by side, Ally in the middle of Matt and Luke, toward the slowly spinning wheel at the center of the fair.

"Six, going on sixteen." Luke's brows wiggled, and when he looked at Amy her heart kerthunked against her rib cage because his eyes sparkled with mischief, just like his daughter's had outside the diner.

"She seemed like a sweetheart to me."

Luke's brows shot up, but his smile was pure paternal pride. His expression did something weird to the muscles in her chest and, as he lifted a hand to run his fingers through his hair, she noted—without meaning to—that he didn't wear a wedding band.

Ally wasn't interested in a relationship. She'd had a handful of disastrous and brief relationships, which had all served to convince her of something she'd known since she was very young: men weren't worth the effort.

This man, handsome or not, would be no different.

Besides, he wasn't the first good-looking guy she'd ever met. He had no business setting her pulse racing like this.

"Ah, Andy!" Matt gestured with a wave to a wiry old man standing right at the bottom of the Ferris wheel, just like Matt had predicted. He put a hand in the small of Ally's back, guiding her forward. She fought a desire to look over her shoulder and make sure Luke was following.

"What's that?" Andy's eyes, obsidian black, lifted from the wheel for a moment, scanning the trio. He tipped his head at Luke before shifting his gaze to Matt. "You call me, son?"

"Yes, sir. This is Amy James. She's not from 'round here.

She's trying to track down a man her mom used to know. Jack Monroe. You heard of him?"

"Monroe, Monroe." He tapped a wiry finger to the side of his chin, and Ally held her breath without meaning to. "Jack Monroe." He began to shake his head a little, and Ally's hope dropped all the way to the cold ground at their feet.

"He'd be in his early fifties," she prompted, her voice a little breathy. "Tall and thin?"

"Not ringing any bells." Andy grunted.

Hope plummeted and Ally felt disappointment threaten tears. "Darn it," she muttered, nodding, trying to smile to show gratitude.

"Monroe, you said?"

New hope burst in her chest. "Yes?"

"Might have been the name of a fella who came through this way ten or so years back. It was a long time ago."

Ally's heart was pounding hard, because the envelope was postmarked more recently than that. If he was here ten years ago, and again a few years ago, wasn't it likely he'd been here the whole time? That he lived here?

"I think he might have gone and got a job in Beauty Falls—at that café just off the highway."

Ally's heart was ready to burst out of her. "Really?"

"Yeah, really." He nodded, and she caught a glimpse of the man he might have been fifty years earlier, before life had forged fault lines on his face, before his eyes had taken on the look of one who'd seen too much life and loss. He was handsome and…kind. The word came to her out of nowhere. She wanted to hug him.

For the first time since getting this harebrained idea into her head, she felt like she was on the brink of discovering her father.

Relief was instantaneous. The kind of relief you felt any time you set out to achieve something and came within sight of your goal. She'd wanted to answer the questions that had dogged her since he'd left. She'd wanted to understand.

And surely if she found him, she'd be able to do that.

And yet…

Success was a double-edged sword because, Ally suspected, in her heart of hearts, that there was nothing he could say to make this better. She couldn't hope for a happily ever after here—just an understanding.

She smiled cautiously at Andy, and his eyes glinted, as though he perhaps understood her ambivalence.

"If you find him, tell him Andy Heyworth says hey. Tell him I hope he's doing well for himself."

Chapter Three

"YOU IN TOWN for long?" Luke watched as Matt disappeared into the crowd, acknowledging a sense of disloyalty because he was glad Matt had left, glad he was alone with this woman.

Ally shook her head, so her ponytail swished a little, shimmering like gold in the reflected glow of the overhead string lights. "I'm not really sure."

"Where are you staying?" Luke hadn't intended to ask the question. He wasn't even sure why he had. They didn't get many tourists, at least, not like this.

Like what?

Attractive?

Okay, she was attractive. She was really, really beautiful, in fact, with flawless skin and honey-blond hair and wide-spaced blue eyes that seemed to linger a little longer than was necessary on his, making him aware for the first time in a long time that he was a man. Not just a dad. Not just the town's resident Mr. Fix-It.

"Cardinal Cottage?"

He nodded, the pretty little rental by the creek a perfect

spot for a tourist. It was named after the state bird, which nested all around the cottage—its distinctive red body and beak a highlight for visitors. "You know your way there okay?"

She smiled up at him, a smile that he could have sworn was teasing. "I mean, I did find my way here okay, so...I think I can follow the breadcrumbs back."

Yes, she was definitely teasing and something sliced through him, because there was flirtation in her words, or maybe he just hoped there was. Either way, it filled him with panic—he hadn't flirted with a woman in a really, really long time. "I'd hate you to get lost, that's all."

"What are you, some kind of welcome wagon? Town spokesperson?" She lifted a single brow, and her face went from sweet to sexy in a nanosecond.

"Just doing my civic duty," Luke volleyed back, his own voice kind of teasing.

"I see." She bit down on her lower lip. His eyes dropped to the gesture, and awareness slammed into him. "Well, thanks for that. Between you and Matt, I've been very well looked after."

It had been a long time since he'd felt desire for a woman, but he recognized it now. And if he hadn't, the healthy zing of jealousy that had rushed over him out of nowhere at her harmless mention of Matt would have made him understand. He was attracted to her. He liked her. That knowledge made his voice come out about an octave deeper than normal. "Glad to hear it." He cleared his throat, a clumsy-feeling smile on his lips.

She tossed a glance over her shoulder toward the field with all the cars. He caught a hint of fragrance. Not perfume, more like soap or conditioner, soft and summery, like lilacs or the old-fashioned roses Nana had let grow all tangled and wild against the side of the house.

Luke couldn't quite put his finger on it, but he was reluctant to say goodbye. Which was stupid. Obviously he had to go back to the fair and find Stella, stop her from infusing her blood with sugar as her uncle Jacob was no doubt allowing her to do at this very minute.

"It's a nice town," she said almost wistfully. Was it possible she didn't want to go, either? Her gaze scraped over his face, and his gut did something weird, like it was being pummeled from the inside out.

"You know, I'll get thrown out if I don't agree with you."

"We can't have that." She lifted a hand to the strap of her bag, pulling it tighter over her shoulder. Another look toward her car and then, "Well, thanks for…" She frowned. "Looking out for me."

Had he done that? "No worries." His eyes dropped to her lips again, and his gut rolled. "I'll see you around."

Was he imagining the way she sucked in a sharp breath?

"Sure." A quick jerk of her head. "See you around."

He watched her until she reached her car, only once she

was inside turning on his heel and moving back to the fair in search of Stella.

ALLY SAT BEHIND the steering wheel, waiting for her breathing to return to normal. She flicked a glance to the rearview mirror, her pulse speeding up as her eyes picked him out even at this distance.

This was *not* why she'd come to Cape Hope. She wasn't here to flirt with some guy, no matter how gorgeous he was. She wasn't here to lose herself in his eyes, no matter how fascinating she found them. She wasn't here to listen to his thick, deep voice, his sexy accent, until her tummy was in knots.

She'd come to Cape Hope to find her father, and she wasn't about to get tied up with a local she'd only know for a week or so. A local who had a daughter, and probably an ex-wife or ex-girlfriend or whatever. Baggage. Complications. Everything she didn't want or need.

With that reassuring thought, she started the engine and pointed the car back toward the road. It was only once she got to Cardinal Cottage that she realized she'd been smiling the whole drive there.

The cottage was just as quaint as the name had made it sound. Small and white with roses growing up one side, though they were barren now, the vines just bracken, but no less charming for that. She could imagine them as they'd be in summer, full of green leaves and blooms, and the odd thorn to remind passersby that nothing of such beauty came without at least the threat of pain.

Sweetgums were at the back of the cottage, so tall they reached to the sky, and winter had robbed them of their plumage, leaving the tree like a bundle of bones exposed to the world. A few Loblolly pines ran down the side of the house, giving it the feeling of the woodcutter's cottage in a fairy tale.

Ally grabbed her bag from the trunk, slung it over her shoulder, and unlocked the door. It was even sweeter at night than it had been that afternoon—a lamp in the hall made the place glow, and at some point the owner had come in to leave a basket in the kitchen. Ally looked through it with a smile still playing about her lips. Preserves, brioche, eggs, and a quart of milk, and maple-smoked bacon in the fridge, as well as some tomatoes and apples.

Closing the fridge, she grabbed a candy bar and went into the living room. Without wasting another moment, she pulled out her laptop and typed "Beauty Falls" into an internet browser.

Excitement trembled inside of her, as well as anxiety.

She'd tried "Jack Monroe" and "North Carolina," but now she typed in "Jack Monroe" and "Beauty Falls" and a heap of results populated the list.

Her hands trembled, and her breath burned in her throat

as she scanned the entries and selected the third one down.

It was a newspaper article from the *New Hanover Gazette*. "Local Man Wins Culinary Contest."

The article went on to describe a cooking contest that brought chefs from all over the country to Beauty Falls, judged by a famous television personality each year. Usually the award went to someone from New York or Washington; this was the first year in its sixty-two-year history that a Beauty Falls entrant had won.

Holding her breath, she skimmed right to the bottom of the article and then made a strangled noise.

Because it was him.

Unmistakably, absolutely, without a single doubt, the face staring back at Ally was that of Jack Monroe.

Her dad.

Tears filled her eyes, and she didn't bother to blink them away. Ally thought of him as he'd been then. Twenty years ago. She had a mental image of him and despite the passage of time, she hadn't known how to update it. Had he gained weight, lost hair, turned gray? No, as it turned out.

Jack Monroe looked much as he ever had. A little older, slim, tall, and unmistakably happy.

A lump formed in her throat as she peered more closely at the screen, her eyes misting up. Because this wasn't the face of a man who was filled with regrets, who lived with heartbreak. And it made her own pain seem even worse, because she was alone in this.

It made her feel foolish, too.

Foolish for coming here when he'd discarded her and moved on. He'd made it clear he didn't want her in his life and yet here she was, turning up like the proverbial bad penny.

She stared at the photo for so long it burned into her retinas.

He was here, just as she'd somehow known he would be when she'd found the envelope. He wasn't dead, nor suffering from some form of amnesia so far as she could tell, nothing that could explain why he'd walked out of her life twenty years ago and not thought of her since.

What had she been expecting?

A better reason for his disappearance? Definitely.

But there wasn't one. At least, there wasn't one she could see. Her dad was alive, living a whole new life—without her.

She put her laptop down and stood up, pacing the small living room floor, fidgeting with her hands. Because she'd come to North Carolina wanting to see her father, needing to know, and now she wasn't even sure she could face him.

Just seeing his picture had unnerved her, had made her heart break all over again. What would it be like in person?

She expelled a shaky breath, pausing for a moment, staring out of the window unseeing. The wind stirred up and one of the large trees overhead scratched its wooded knuckles over the roof. She barely heard it.

Jack Monroe.

Chef.

Just like she'd grown up to be.

She closed her eyes, and she was five years old again, cracking eggs into a bowl under his expert tutelage, careful not to get shell into the mix, concentrating so hard she poked the tip of her tongue from the corner of her lips.

She was a child, learning to whisk, froth, stir, fold.

She was six and he was gone.

Her heart pounded against her rib cage. She turned back to her laptop, staring at it suspiciously.

She'd come a long way to learn the truth; she wasn't going to fall at the last hurdle. In the morning, she'd go to Beauty Falls.

In the morning, she'd go and find the man who'd broken her heart, who'd taught her that the only person you could ever really count on was yourself.

A STORM HAD stirred itself to life out over the Atlantic and, as the new day dawned, it rushed toward land, so Ally woke to the sound of heavy rain hitting the roof. She lay in bed a moment, staring out at the scenery that was so different than what she was familiar with—pine trees swaying, mist embracing their bristled bodies, before remembering, with a thud, all that had happened the night before.

She remembered what she'd promised herself as she'd

fallen asleep—that she'd go to Beauty Falls and find him. *Today.*

And for someone who'd driven cross-country with this exact purpose in mind, she approached the task with a heavy sense of dread, dressing warmly—jeans, a sweater, and a trench coat with a hood, which she pulled up to cover her hair. Boots were by the entrance to the cottage; she slid them on and pulled the door shut without grabbing breakfast.

She locked the door behind her with the big old key—no doubt locals didn't bother but, while you could take the girl out of the city, it was harder to take the city out of the girl.

Drawing in a succession of deep breaths, she set her phone up with the navigation and put on her favorite playlist, the familiarity of a Dixie Chicks song just what she needed to keep her calm. Calmish, anyway. No. Not at all calm.

She drove slowly through town, telling herself she wasn't deliberately keeping an eye out for a certain broad-shouldered man and his blond-haired accomplice.

The road was winding and took all her concentration, particularly as the rain continued to fall, heavy and drenching. Forests were on one side of her car and on the other, houses, but not many and with lots of land between. Farm houses, country homes, beautiful and old with wraparound balconies, the kinds of places that the South was renowned for.

Before she'd come across the envelope, she'd never had

much inclination to visit this part of the world. Europe, yes. In particular, Paris—for someone who'd always adored French cuisine, it was a must-see. But the little towns that dotted the east coast? They weren't on her radar at all.

And yet…

As her Prius ate up the miles, she couldn't help but admit this scenery held a timeless appeal. The forest to her left with pine trees that looked a mile high was just the kind of place she might have liked to lose herself in, come summer. Pack a picnic and a good book and weave through those thick trunks until she was far from the road and people and interruptions. She'd stay there, staring up at what she could see of the sky through the bristly treetops.

She bet there'd be bluebells, too, carpeting the ground underfoot.

She wouldn't be here to see that, though. By the time summer realized it was missed and came to bathe North Carolina in shining warmth, Ally would be back in Wisconsin, far away from here.

Far away from her father.

She ground her teeth together as she summoned every self-protective instinct she possessed—anger, disbelief, fury, hurt. The hurt that had spread like oil through her whole childhood—all her life—so even the good memories were tainted now by the knowledge that how much she'd loved him was one-sided. By the knowledge that her own father was capable of picking up and leaving her.

The pine trees were still thick at her side as she passed the town's welcome sign. "Welcome to Beauty Falls!" it declared in happy, red script. Beneath it, blocked in black: Population, 4,900.

Slowing down, she continued straight on until a sign indicated "right" for the Town Center. Turning into it, consulting the map, she slowed further, crawling up the main street until she saw something that jerked at her brain.

Cup of Joe.

More memories slammed against her. Memories of waking up and hearing her father pronounce, "Cup of Joe time."

Her lips formed a grim line on her face, her skin not much darker than freshly fallen snow. She pulled the car into a space and sat there a long time, just staring. Looking at what she could see of the café from here, which was, admittedly, not a lot.

It glowed warm, hardly difficult given the bleak gray of the day, and a sign out front proclaimed, "Best Coffee for Miles!" Beneath that, on the same sign, "Award-Winning Food!" and she saw the photograph in her mind's eye, she saw her dad, and suddenly she was galvanized into action.

Pulling the hood of her trench coat back into place, she stepped out of the car, moving toward the café almost as though she were being propelled by some unknown force. Puddles were underfoot; she didn't care.

She moved swiftly up the porch steps, pausing at the entrance as an older man came out. He nodded at her and held the door. She pushed into the café, breath held, looking around.

The first thing that struck her was that it was surprisingly busy. A real little haunt for locals, every table was occupied and there was a line at the register. Christmas was alive here as it had been in the diner in Cape Hope. A tree set up in one corner glistened with brightly colored lights, and tinsel garlands were looped from beam to beam, making the whole room look festive and merry. Carols played over the speakers, old jazz ones that had always been her personal favorites.

She took a seat at the counter, grabbing a newspaper and pretending to read while surreptitiously continuing to scan the café's interior.

"Can I help you?"

She turned to face the waitress, a girl in her late teens with curly brown hair and a kind smile and a name tag that read Benita. Ally nodded. "Just a coffee with cream, thanks."

"You sure you don't want a *pain aux raisins*? They're straight outta the oven."

Ally's stomach groaned hungrily, protesting the fact she'd skipped breakfast, and she laughed softly. "You twisted my arm."

"I'm good at that." The girl winked. "I haven't seen you in here before. Are you from here?"

Ally's heart pounded at the lie she'd already offered to a few people, a lie that had been invented for this very moment. "No," she said hesitantly. "I'm just passing through."

"What brings you to Beauty Falls?"

"I'm...looking for an old friend of my mom's."

"Well, this is the place to find someone. Just about everyone in town crosses through here most days." She wiped a smudge off the corner of the counter. "I'm Benita."

Ally swallowed. "Amy. Amy James."

"Just holler if you need help finding your mom's friend," Benita offered, writing something on her notepad and sliding the order slip into a window.

Ally followed the action, about to ask about Jack Monroe, when she froze in her stool, her mouth clamped shut all of a sudden.

A hand came out to take the order slip. An arm. And even though it was just a limb, nothing much really, she *knew.*

She stared at the window, waiting impatiently until a plate was put up. Jack Monroe's head craned out and it was like being punched in her belly. The photos of him she'd found on the internet had shown how he'd changed, but looking at him now, what she noticed was how the same he still he was, how exactly like the dad she remembered. Oh, he was older, but his eyes, his smile, his face—he was her father, unmistakably. "Order up, hon."

Ally's stomach had a million butterflies. *Hon.* He'd called her that. And her mom.

Years ago. When they weren't fighting—which wasn't often.

She knew she should stop staring, but she couldn't. She couldn't tear her eyes away.

The tone of his voice was a building block of her DNA so it sparked a lavalike torrent of recognition through her body. And a thousand memories rained down on her. She swept her eyes shut, listening, but she wasn't here anymore. She was back in their home, sitting on his lap, watching television while he drank beer. She was a kid again, and he was her world.

After so many years, across a busy little café, separated by a wall and through a window, she had absolutely no doubt. It was her dad.

Tears welled inside of her, filling her throat, her eyes, salt exploding through her body, and she jerked out of her chair, nerves firing through her.

She shouldn't have come.

What had she thought? That she'd see him and suddenly it would all make sense? Was there *any* explanation he could offer that would make this okay?

He'd deserted her.

Abandoned her.

Disappeared from her life as though she meant nothing to him, as though she was worthless. And that feeling of worthlessness had stalked her ever since.

With a muffled groan, she spun and weaved back through the restaurant, pushing through the door as though fire was licking the soles of her feet.

"Ma'am? Ma'am? Your coffee?"

The voice followed her, but Ally didn't stop.

She couldn't.

She was afraid she was going to be sick. Nausea possessed her gut.

She ran back across the road, startling as a truck came around the corner and had to brake abruptly to avoid hitting her. She held her hand up in silent apology but didn't stop running until she was in the safety of her little car. She started the engine and turned onto the road, driving as fast as was safe, needing to get the heck out of Dodge.

On the way back to Cape Hope, she didn't notice a thing about the scenery. She barely noticed the way the clouds drifted apart to show expanses of crystal-clear blue; she barely noticed the way the absence of rain meant the presence of birds, nor the way they swooped merrily from one side of the road to the other, nor the curious little white-tailed fawn that came to the side of the road as she passed, watching her journey with deep brown eyes.

She'd seen him, and her whole body was in a state of anxiety. Her brow was dotted with perspiration, her hands trembled, her throat felt thick, her eyes stung.

She drove to Cape Hope as though an invisible string was pulling her there and, despite her state of unease, as she turned onto the main street, her breathing slowed a little, and her fingers stopped trembling so badly.

Spontaneously, she pulled into a space out the front of

Tucker's Diner, staring at it for several seconds in the hope it would push thoughts of Cup of Joe from her mind. People moved in and out of the diner, going about their lives, with no idea Ally was sitting in the car trying to stave off a panic attack.

She dipped her head forward, pressing it to the wheel of the car. She was glad of one thing, and one thing only: that no one knew who she really was.

Seeing her father had shown her how ambivalent she was about this. When she'd left Wisconsin, she'd simply been acting on instincts. She'd had a lead on the man she'd lost so long ago. But having lost him once didn't mean he was worthy of being found. It sure as hell didn't mean he deserved to be in her life. Her stomach looped uncomfortably as she remembered his face, the way it had been just a half hour ago, his smile, his eyes, everything so *damned familiar.*

And if somehow, someone had known who she was, and happened to mention to Jack Monroe that she was looking for him? Her stomach squeezed again, like she was on an enormous roller coaster, flying down a sharp hill. Then this decision would be taken out of her hands. She'd be as powerless now as she'd been then—he'd be able to take her or leave her.

This wasn't his decision. He didn't get to choose. She did.

So she was Amy James until she was ready to admit to being Ally Monroe. *If.*

Maybe she never would. Maybe she'd been stupid to attempt this. Maybe she should just keep driving out of Cape Hope, away from North Carolina, and pretend this never happened.

Except…

She lifted her head, her eyes landing on the diner once more. In the same way she'd acted on instincts when she'd come to Cape Hope, instincts were telling her to stay. That she was here now and that nothing good came from being hasty.

What she needed was a coffee. Coffee would help her make sense of this. Coffee would soothe her frazzled nerves. Maybe even one of the beautiful pastries she'd been eyeing the day before. With a fortifying breath, she stepped out of the car and through the street before pushing into the warmth of the diner.

A young man was behind the counter. He smiled as Ally approached, but she was too distracted to offer much more than a cursory lift of her lips.

"Hey." She scanned the cabinet. "A coffee with cream, thanks, and a muffin to go." She handed over her reusable to-go cup from inside her bag.

"We've got raspberry, blueberry, chocolate chip, vanilla, gluten-free carrot…"

"Raspberry's fine." The words came out terse; she grimaced but didn't apologize. She was too scattered. Every time she closed her eyes for even a millisecond, she saw him.

"Raspberry. No problem." He moved slowly to the cabinet, fumbling as he lifted out a bag and separated it with tongs before reaching into the pantry and pulling the muffin out. Ally resisted an impulse to tap her fingertips on the counter. Seriously, the guy couldn't have moved slower if he'd tried.

"You're new in town?" he drawled as he handed the muffin over and moved to the coffee machine.

It was easy to deliver the same line she'd offered the young waitress in Beauty Falls. "I'm just passing through."

"It's not really tourist season."

"No," she agreed, softening her tone with effort, thinking longingly of the privacy of the cottage she'd rented. She needed to think—she needed to get all this straight in her head.

Her mom would have killed her for being here. *"He's just a bad person, sweetie. Some people are rotten apples and I'm sorry to say your daddy's one of them."*

"I guess there's the fair," he continued, apparently oblivious to how uninterested Ally was in having this conversation.

"Yes," she agreed crisply and, to avoid the need for any further conversation, she moved away from the counter altogether, looking at one wall of the diner that was covered in simple black Sharpie drawings against the crisp white paint. Closer inspection showed that they were townspeople—clever sketches that caught their likenesses, even in the crude, simple line drawings. She saw Andy Heyworth's picture and recognized him instantly, even though he looked younger and more spry in this representation. A little further down, there was a man with his arm around a pregnant woman, and in her belly there was a star.

Curiosity had her leaning closer and her breath snagged as something in the man's bearing made her heart beat speed up. Luke Miller? And his wife? Pregnant with Stella?

Curiosity sparked and another mystery began to tease her, to tempt her to ignore her own disastrous morning and focus on something else.

But it was still too fresh and raw, and she was too stricken by the step she'd taken to really think of anything else. She blinked and saw her father—as he was now—like the new memory was overwriting any of the old ones she'd held on to for so long. He was no longer a figment of her imagination, a "what if" in her life. He was a living, breathing man in the next town over.

She'd found him, just as she'd set out to do.

And she had no earthly idea what came next.

Chapter Four

CARDINAL COTTAGE WAS not quite the scenic little beauty she'd left earlier that morning.

In some ways it was even more idyllic, with fingers of mist cradling it in the palms of their inclement hands, clouds breathing past the fogged windows. The hall still glowed golden, and there was a potbelly stove in the living room that she was itching to light, but, unfortunately, more urgent things required her attention first. Stalking into the kitchen to pull a plate out on which to place her muffin, she almost slipped onto her *derriere* when her sock-clad foot connected with a big puddle of water on the tiled floor.

"Shoot!" Ally steadied herself on the back of a chair, yanking her back painfully to stop from going over. A quick inspection showed the ceiling had sprung a leak. It was no surprise. The rain was falling hard and heavy, and this cottage was ancient.

Muffin forgotten, she fished in her pocket for her cell and dialed the cottage owner's number. Isabella Hough had shown Ally through the property the day before and made sure Ally had everything she could need for her stay.

She was alarmed to hear of the leak and promised help would be with Ally immediately. "Sit tight, darlin'. Thanks for letting me know."

Ally hung up, wondering what else she was supposed to have done—ignore the worsening puddle and pooling ceiling?—and tiptoed around the puddle to grab a plate before doing exactly what Isabella had suggested: wait.

She nibbled at the muffin distractedly, staring at the raindrops falling into the kitchen, thinking it was no less pretty for being an accidental water feature.

It wasn't long before the sound of gravel crunching under tires heralded the arrival of "help." Ally stood, wiping her fingers together to dust off the crumbs before moving gingerly through the kitchen and toward the cottage door.

Yanking it open, she had the brief impression of a red pickup swinging alongside her Prius. She waited, hip propped on the door frame, but at the sight of who stepped out of the vehicle and cast his eyes over the little cottage, her heart backflipped over itself in excitement. She quashed the reaction as best she could but, darn it, not completely. How could she?

Luke Miller swaggered—yeah, he definitely swaggered—toward the little cottage. He was wearing distressed denims, but not fashionably aged, just faded from use, with a black T-shirt beneath an old black leather jacket. As he got out of the pickup he grabbed a canvas bag from the trunk, swinging it over his shoulder, and dipping his head forward as he moved to the door. "Hey." He grinned as he approached and, despite the mixed-up morning she'd had, she smiled back like it was the most natural thing in the world. "You've got a leak?" he prompted when she didn't say anything, and heat colored her cheeks because she was pretty sure she'd been staring.

"Oh, yeah." She frowned, so a little line formed between her brows. "You're the handyman?"

"When I'm not the town's volunteer firefighter." He grinned and Ally couldn't help but feel a buzz in her stomach at that—the idea of this guy running into burning buildings in his spare time, to save the town's residents.

"Sorry to bother you on a day like this."

"It's clearing," he said. "Besides, it's my job. In the kitchen, Izzie said?"

"Yeah." Belatedly, she realized she'd left him standing in the rain. She pushed up from the door frame and moved deeper into the cottage. "This way."

It was the first time she'd seen him *in a house*, or indoors, surrounded by walls and a ceiling, and all it did was make Ally feel like she was Alice in Wonderland and she'd gone through the looking glass.

She was tiny, the house was tiny, and he was…huge. Easily over six feet, broadly muscled, strong, outdoorsy. She looked at his hands as he placed his bag on one of the kitchen chairs, capable and broad, tanned fingers with a sprinkling of coarse hair on each knuckle.

"Did you wake up to this?"

"I... No." She frowned again. "I don't know. I went out early this morning. I didn't come in here." Of course the leak must have been there, and if she'd only made a coffee for the drive, she'd have seen it and been able to get someone onto fixing it earlier.

"You went out voluntarily? This morning?" He lifted his brows, and her heart stammered. Warning was in her awareness of this man—she didn't do this. She avoided handsome, nice guys. She avoided the complications and the expectations, the fake promises, all of it.

"Yeah. Why?"

"It was quite a storm."

"Oh, right, I know. I wanted to check out Beauty Falls."

"Ah." He nodded, reaching into his bag, pulling out a small metallic tool. "That's right. The mysterious friend of your mom's?"

"Right." It took an extreme effort to act nonchalant—casual, even—at the reference to her dad. But there was no way Ally had any intention of telling another soul what she was really doing in Cape Hope.

"Did you find him?"

"No." An image of her dad flashed before her eyes, so she had to spin away from Luke to stop him from seeing her reaction. She felt his eyes on her back and moved to the other side of the kitchen, away from the leak and the sinkhole that was Luke Miller's appeal.

"Things are about to get messy in here," he said, and when she turned around he was throwing down floor coverings. "You might want to grab a drink and head out."

"Oh, sure." Heat bloomed in her cheeks because she'd honestly been planning to pull up a seat and watch him work. She filled a glass with water, moving to the door. "Do you need anything?"

He turned to her and their eyes met and something exploded inside her belly—desire. She recognized it instantly and it made her knees tremble and her blood simmer.

He stood there, staring at her, something in his bearing making her wonder if he was feeling exactly what she was, his throat moving as he swallowed, so her eyes dropped to his lips, then to the square, stubbled jaw beneath. "I'm fine."

She frowned, trying to focus on their conversation. "You're fine?"

He nodded, a smile flicking on his lips. "I don't need anything."

"Right." She nodded jerkily and stepped backward. "Okay. I'll just be"—she waved vaguely toward the living room—"in there."

HE TAPED THE tarp down over the roof, trying not to think about Amy James inside the cottage.

He tried not to think about how adorable she'd looked

when she'd opened the door, surprise evident in her pretty features as she'd eaten him up with her eyes. Tried not to think about the way she'd stared at him like he was some kind of ice cream, brought to life.

Tried not to think about the fact that, for the first time since Jen had died, he was looking at another woman and feeling all the things.

Desire, amusement, interest, fascination, lust, attraction.

Everything.

It was all zipping through him, and it had been so long since he'd felt *any* of those things, let alone all of them at once, that he had no clue how to act around her, how to speak, or what to do.

In another world, if he didn't have a kid and a history and all the baggage, he'd have simply asked her to dinner. He'd have liked to take her to dinner, to see her dressed up, and to sit across from her and watch as she sipped wine and used those expressive hands of hers to tell stories. He'd have liked to know more about her—he'd have liked to know everything about her.

He snapped the corner of the tarp into place, then crouched back a little, in no hurry to get off the roof of the cottage even as the rain began to fall a little heavier. He checked his handiwork, making sure it would hold even if the storm blew up again.

It was watertight—or as good as he'd be able to get it until he could organize the roofing supplies to be brought into town.

The thing was, he didn't date. It wasn't that he hadn't had opportunity. There weren't that many single guys in Cape Hope, and he'd seen the way women looked at him. He'd been asked out, he'd been hit on, he'd been propositioned for indecent, secret assignations that had made him chuckle as he'd turned them down—he wasn't really a "mess around in a motel" kind of man.

Up until Amy James and her little electric car had driven into town, he hadn't been even the slightest bit interested.

He'd loved Jen, and Jen had died. Therefore, his heart and libido and everything that went along with that had died with her—he had no use for them again. Simple.

How did single parents even do the whole dating thing?

It wasn't just about him; there was Stella to consider. She was his life. He could never go out with someone who didn't adore her, and vice versa. So did dating as a single dad mean involving Stella in some way? He had no idea—it was something he hadn't given even a moment's thought to until today.

He eased back a little, moving carefully over the roof until he felt the ladder propped against the gutter. He took a step down, then another, until he was on the ground. Rain was falling harder now, making pinging noises against their cars. He dipped his head forward and walked quickly toward the cottage door.

Shrugging out of his jacket and hanging it on the hook,

he ran a hand through his hair, drying it off as best he could as he kicked off his boots. He kind of wished he'd worn nicer socks, he thought as he moved deeper into the cottage.

She was standing in the living room, surrounded by smoke.

"Jeez, Amy, a flood's not enough?" He was grinning. "You want to smoke the place out now, too?"

She spun around, fanning her face, her consternation unmistakable. His gut clenched hard. Yeah, he was lost to this, and that was definitely not a good thing. He moved across the room quickly, throwing open the little French doors that led to a brick courtyard, then moved to the fire. "It's cold," she explained needlessly. "I thought it'd be easy."

"These old pot bellies can be temperamental," he said reassuringly, opening the door and crouching down on his haunches. "And you've got about a ton too much paper in here."

"I thought paper would make it catch quicker."

He tilted his head up, his eyes locking to hers, and something like sparks exploded between them. "Don't tell me you've never lit a fire?"

She frowned and, for some reason, he was reminded of Stella, that same fierce burst of pride that made her hate admitting mistakes crossing Amy James's face. "I've seen it done plenty of times."

He smothered his laugh. "Not quite like this, though." He grabbed the gloves in the basket above the fire and pushed them onto his hands, reaching in and removing at least an armful of newspaper, carrying it to the courtyard and placing it on the grass. He stomped on it then, staying just long enough to make sure the rain did a good enough job putting any sparks out before heading back inside.

She was trying to light it again, and he stood back, watching, somehow knowing she wanted to do this herself, without his help. This time, flames licked at the paper left in there, and he had the satisfaction of seeing her stand up, eyeing the fire with obvious pride. "Ta-da!"

Her pleasure was contagious. He smiled wide. "You did it."

"I just put too much paper in," she said, but the words were hoarse. "How's the leak?" She was all business.

"The roof's patched." He moved to stand in front of the fire. It brought him close to Amy, though, closer than he'd intended. If she shifted, just a fraction, they'd be touching.

She didn't. She stayed where she was, hands extended toward the heat. "So you're all done?"

"I'll have to come back and work on the ceiling again, once I've got the supplies in." He could have sworn he saw something like relief cross her face. His gut did a funny little roll. This was not a good sign. "Maybe I should take your number? Just to make sure I come at a good time?"

Her eyes jerked to his and, after a tiny pause—a pause in which his breath stayed locked in his lungs—she nodded. "Yeah, okay." Her teeth sunk into her lower lip and her furrowed brow showed she was surprised by her acquiescence to this.

Before she could change her mind, he pulled his phone out of his pocket and handed it to her. She took it after a slight hesitation, and their fingers brushed in a way that made his blood warm and his mind go in a direction that he instinctively wanted to ignore.

He watched as she input her number and saved it as "Amy." Her eyes lifted to his, a ton of emotion in their depths that birthed a million questions in him—questions he wanted answers to but didn't know how to ask. "So I know you're not from these parts," he said, sliding his phone into his back pocket with the appearance of nonchalance. He strode toward the kitchen, where his tools were still set up. "Where are you from?"

She walked behind him. "Madison, Wisconsin."

"You're a long way from home."

"I know. I drove it." She was teasing him again, just like the night before at the fair, and it had the same impact. His stomach pulled, and amusement warred with stark desire.

"This friend of your mom's must be pretty special to you."

"I don't really know him." Her voice hitched a little at the admission and speculation gave way to curiosity.

"Special to your mom then?"

Amy lifted her slender shoulders, her expression blanked of emotion in a way he suspected to be forced. "My mom died. A bit over six months ago." She looked away from him, her face in profile taut, tense. "I guess I just wanted to tie up some loose ends."

Sympathy rushed through him. "I'm sorry. About your mom."

She nodded, clearly not welcoming this conversation. "I never know what to say to that. I guess 'thanks.'"

He smiled, despite the serious tenor of the conversation. "I feel exactly the same. When my wife died, people would come up to me in the street and say, 'condolences' or 'you're in my prayers' and they'd be so worried about me, scared I might break or something, I'd find myself comforting them, assuring them I was fine, that I would be fine."

"I didn't know she'd died." Amy swiveled back to look at him, her own face a reflection of the same sympathy they'd just been disavowing. "When?"

And despite the fact he didn't talk about Jen often—he didn't need to, everyone he knew also knew the story, knew what had happened or had been there at the time—he found himself saying, "Six years ago. In childbirth."

She let out a soft breath, shaking her head. "I'm so sorry." And then she winced. "Sorry. Again." She shook her head impatiently. "I can't imagine how hard that must have been for you."

"Yeah." He nodded, the sting of that night one that would never leave his soul. It burned into his being, branded like the hide of a cow. "It was like that Dickens quote, you know? The best of times, the worst of times? I mean, nothing beats holding your kid for the first time. And, even at birth, Stella was fierce. She was cross and impatient and completely her own little soul, ready to take on the world. I looked at her strength and couldn't believe she could be so alive and vibrant at the same time Jen was just…gone. I can't explain it."

Lightning cracked outside the window, illuminating the room with silver light. Amy jumped. "What happened? With your wife?"

"A stroke during delivery. It led to a massive brain bleed—all within minutes. There was nothing that could be done. Nothing I could do." He ground his teeth together, hating that even now.

"I can't think of much worse. I'm so sorry."

He jerked his head. "Thanks." The word was gruff. He turned to look at her, scanning her face. "What about your mom?"

She chewed on her lip thoughtfully and, when she shifted now, it was quite spontaneous, but it brought her body closer to his so warmth flooded his limbs. "A heart attack. It was sudden, too. No warning. No time to say goodbye." Amy's expression crumpled. "She was so young. Too young to die. And we never had any idea." She lifted her face to his, and the depth of her grief made him wish he knew her better, so he could put an arm around her and pull her closer to him. "She hadn't been sick. She was healthy and fit. It just came out of nowhere."

He made a sound of sympathy. "That must have been hard for you and your family."

A hollowness haunted the depths of her eyes. "I don't have any family." The words were said firmly, but his heart hurt for her admission. "It's just me now."

"So you came looking for someone else who knew your mom?"

"Yeah." Her voice wobbled and her jaw tightened. With determination? "I guess."

"I hope you find him, Amy." And he did. He wanted her to succeed so there was someone else she could talk to about her mom, share her memories with. Whoever this friend was, he obviously mattered a heap to her if she'd driven across the country to locate him.

Thunder grumbled overhead. Amy shuddered.

"You don't like storms?"

Her expression was self-deprecating. "Not particularly."

It was surprising, this admission of vulnerability. He ran his gaze over her face for a moment, wanting to offer to stay with her and keep her company. But she was already straightening, slipping away from him physically and emotionally.

"Thanks for coming so quickly to fix the, um, leak." She pointed to the ceiling, where he'd used a Sharpie to square off a big patch of drywall that would need cutting and replacing.

"No problem. I'll call you before I come back, okay?"

"Great." Her voice was definitely husky. It did funny things to his gut. The desire to stay increased.

"See you later."

"Uh-huh."

She didn't walk him to the door, and he was glad, because the urge to do something really stupid and ask her out was almost overwhelming him now. He grabbed his coat off the hook and strode out in the rain to his pickup, pulling the heavy driver's door open and sliding into the warmth of the cab.

Only once he started the engine did he chance a look toward the kitchen windows.

She was there, looking out, watching him. Their eyes connected, and a sinking feeling opened up in the pit of his stomach. Because try as he might, Luke had a feeling he was fighting a losing battle, and he didn't much like to lose.

IT MADE SENSE to eat at the diner. Given the last few failed culinary efforts, he could do without a fight over meal quality with Stella. "Okay, butterfly. What's it to be?"

She wrinkled her nose, studying the menu exaggeratedly, even though she ordered the same thing every time. She lifted it a little closer, scanning the contents, and he waited, a smile flickering on his lips. "Cheeseburger and fries," she said, so earnestly.

"For a change?" he couldn't resist teasing.

She poked her tongue out, but she smiled.

"Sit tight. I'll go order." There wasn't much of a line. He was served almost right away. He placed their order then moved back to the table. Stella was folding her napkin over and over again. "How was school?"

"You already asked me that."

"Did I?"

"Yep."

"I forgot. So? How was it?"

She rolled her eyes. "You mean you weren't listening?"

Quite possibly. He'd found it pretty hard to concentrate all day. He kept seeing Amy James and wishing he could turn back time and return to Cardinal Cottage. He kept wondering about her, thinking of questions he wished he'd asked, making a mental note for next time. "Tell me again."

"There's nothing to tell. It was boring."

"Boring, huh?" He arched a brow in disbelief. "Even with that storm?"

"That's *why* it was boring. We weren't allowed to go outside. We had to play in the library."

"So? Books. That's fun."

She compressed her lips. "You don't get it."

"Get what?"

She opened her mouth to speak, but their burgers arrived, and whatever she'd been about to say was lost in that moment.

"Stella?"

"Nothing."

It didn't seem like nothing. "Baby, if something's bothering you, you know you can tell me."

Her chin jutted out defiantly, and love burst through him; love for his strong, determined daughter. "Nothing's bothering me."

"I don't know if I believe you," he said gently.

She glared at him and then looked away, focusing her attention across the restaurant. "I'm tired."

He frowned. That wasn't like Stella. "Eat up. We'll get you home soon."

She wasn't kidding about the whole tiredness thing. It was only three miles from the diner to home, but halfway there, Stella fell asleep in her seat, her little head bobbing to the side. Luke watched her in the rearview mirror when he pulled up at the lights.

Parenting was one of the hardest things he'd ever done, and one of the most rewarding. Sometimes Stella made him want to rip his hair out, and others, his heart practically burst out of him with love and pride.

He felt a hint of disloyalty in being glad that she was asleep, though, glad for a night they wouldn't argue over bedtime and teeth and books and nightmares. Glad for a night to himself to think about the day he'd had.

He settled her in bed and then went into the garage,

working on the porch swing he was making as a Christmas present for Stella, to replace the one that had broken a few years earlier in a huge storm. He worked on the swing for hours, massaging it with his hands, massaging out the knots, sanding it until it was smooth and soft. All the while he thought of Amy and her mysterious blue eyes, the smile she seemed to work overtime to hold back, the feeling he had that she was pushing him away even as there was something about her dragging him closer.

He thought about Amy and, when he fell asleep, she filled his dreams, haunting him with her husky voice and the way she chewed distractingly on her lower lip.

Chapter Five

SHE REALLY HADN'T intended to end up back here. It wasn't like she'd woken up with this place in mind. She'd set out into Cape Hope's Main Street to pick up supplies, only she'd kept driving. She'd simply steered the car, and before she knew it, pine forests were to her left and rambling rural fields to her right.

She drove past the welcome sign to Beauty Falls with an expression of determination that the wait staff at the restaurant she worked at knew to fear. It meant business—*she* meant business. Ally parked a little way from Cup of Joe today, deciding to walk instead. To give herself time to change her mind? Or to psych herself into this?

She couldn't say.

But she was glad she had a few extra minutes up her sleeve. She walked slowly down the street, pulling her trench coat more firmly around her shoulders. Elm trees swept the rooftops, big and spindly in the thrall of the season.

A couple came wandering out of a store, hand in hand, and she slowed for a moment, trying to imagine what that must feel like.

Love. Intimacy.

Ally had never been in love, nor had she ever trusted anyone enough to get up close and personal. Ally liked companionship. She had enough friends. But when it came to men, she preferred to keep a safe distance.

When she was fifteen and in a rebellious stage, her mom had sent her to see a shrink. In hindsight, it had been a good idea—Ally had been pretty untamable and bent on self-destruction.

The shrink, Dr. Hollis, had sagely pointed out that it was little surprise Ally had trust issues. *"Your dad abandoned you. He was the one man you thought you could always count on. Your first love. And he up and disappeared. You're acting out now, Alicia, so you can rationalize your emotional distance. It's easy to throw your hands in the air and say people don't like you when you're acting in a way that's inherently unlikable."*

She'd glowered through the session, convinced her mom was wasting her money.

Nearly a decade later, she kind of thought she might owe Dr. Hollis an apology email. Maybe there was something to what he'd said. She had made emotional distance an art form. Her last relationship had ended almost a year ago. He'd been a sous chef in the restaurant and he'd been fired for stealing.

She had great taste. Not.

Ally stopped walking, propped beside the mailbox, her eyes trained on the café. It was bustling again. She watched the comings and goings for a minute, then moved closer—so close she could see people through the windows, sipping coffee at the counter, laughing, chatting, going about their day.

Sucking in a deep breath, she dipped her head and moved across the street, up the steps and into the café. Noise surrounded her like a blanket, but panic was there, too, suffocating her, making breathing difficult. She weaved through the tables toward the counter, digging her fingernails into her palm to stop herself from being foolish.

Unfortunately, the same girl was serving as had been there the first time Ally had come to the café. Embarrassment had her dipping her head slightly in an instinctive attempt to avoid making eye contact. It was futile, though.

"You're back."

Heat bloomed in her cheeks. "Yeah. I'm sorry I had to run out last time. Something came up."

The waitress waved a hand, like it didn't matter, then pulled a pen from behind her ear and a notebook from her apron pocket. "These things happen. What'll it be?"

Ally scanned the counter, her nerves firing wildly. "Do you have a menu?" Her voice trembled a little.

"Sure." The waitress handed over a laminated sheet of paper.

Ally scanned it quickly without really reading it at first. With a deep breath, she steadied herself a little, scanning the words once more, and settling on corn fritters and bacon.

"Good choice. That's what I'll be having later, too.

They're delicious." She wrote the order down and gestured to the restaurant. "Grab a seat where you can. I'll bring it over when it's ready."

Ally chose a table against the far wall, but with a good view of the kitchen. She leafed through a magazine, but every few moments her eyes would lift back to the kitchen, looking for the man who'd been her dad.

When the young waitress appeared with the corncakes a little while later, she still hadn't seen him. A woman's slim, dark hands were sliding the plates through the server window. But it was only a matter of time, surely. So she waited and she watched and tried to ignore the kaleidoscope of butterflies that were taking over her central nervous system.

She ate the corncakes, and a sledge of strong memories spun through her, like a spider's web in which she had been trapped. There was something familiar about these corncakes, an early taste memory, and though she had no specific recollection of ever having eaten them, she was absolutely certain her dad must have made them for her as a girl.

For Ally's eleventh birthday, her mom had organized a party at the local rec center. It had a pool and high diving board, and Ally had insisted she would jump right off the highest level. She'd climbed up and went to the edge, unprepared for how shaky it would feel and how far away the water would seem. She'd stood there, every movement, every breath, causing the board to quiver alarmingly beneath her. Her stomach had plummeted, and she'd backed away, carefully edging toward the ladder until the nausea passed. She'd contemplated going back down to the pool, to admitting her mom had been right, and it *was* terrifying to imagine jumping off that darn board.

But she hadn't wanted to admit defeat.

More than that, she'd wanted the thrill of doing the dive. And so she'd edged her way out again, stood at the end, more terrified than she'd ever been in her life. She'd closed her eyes, taken one last step, and then she was flying through the air, her body like a dart, careening toward the pool's surface. She'd opened her eyes halfway down, spinning into a proper dive position as best she could, and she'd laughed just before she'd hit the water, because she'd *done it*, and no one could take that away from her.

It had been the best feeling ever, a total rush.

She'd faced her fears and overcome them, and she was going to do it again.

Before she could second-guess herself, she lifted her fingers in the air, silently drawing the waitress's attention.

"You need something, ma'am?"

Ally shook her head, swallowing past the lump in her throat, telling herself to be brave. She'd driven across country to do this—there was no point in putting it off. "These are great. Is the chef around?" Her voice hummed and buzzed in her ears. "I'd love to get the recipe."

"Chefs don't share recipes." The waitress laughed, leaning forward conspiratorially. "But I will tell you there's cayenne pepper in there. Just a sprinkle."

She winked, and impatience burst through Ally. "Right. Well, can I see him? To tell him how great they are?"

The waitress seemed bent on thwarting Ally, though. "He already knows." Ally's insides hummed with the force of her frustration. Before she could find another way to ask to speak to her own damned dad, the waitress smiled kindly and said, "He's not here today, anyway. It's his weekend."

"Oh." Disappointment was a blade slicing through her sides. She flicked her gaze down to the corncakes, trying to hide the strong surge of feelings from the waitress. "Next time."

"Sure." The waitress grinned. "Need anything else?"

"No, thanks." Without intending it, her attention shifted back to the kitchen window. Her dad wasn't here today. She couldn't talk to him. Not now.

But soon.

If she'd had any doubt about whether or not she wanted to confront him, the visceral disappointment she'd felt today upon discovering he wasn't at work showed her how she really felt.

She'd traveled across the country to speak to him and soon—as soon as possible—she would.

CAPE HOPE WAS a seaside town, though the main street was

set about a mile away from the ocean. After leaving Beauty Falls, Ally pulled up in the busy little street, grabbed her reusable takeout cup from the seat beside her, and pushed into the diner, ordering a coffee.

While her drink was being made, she gravitated toward the wall, looking at the pictures again, picking out other faces she thought she recognized from the fair, or from around town, before ending up in front of Luke and the woman she now knew he'd been married to.

She frowned, studying the picture, wondering how an artist could be so clever as to capture a person's essence with just a few simple lines. There was a strength and laconic curiosity in Luke's drawing that was so exactly like him, Ally smiled without realizing it as she studied the illustration.

"Amy?"

She blinked, turning around to see the guy from behind the coffee machine walking toward her, cup in hand.

"Your head was in the clouds. Here's the coffee."

"Thanks. This is a cool mural."

"Yeah." He nodded. "I guess it is. I don't really notice it anymore." He pointed to a picture of a boy. "That's me."

"You've grown since then," she observed with a smile.

He laughed. "Yeah. I was maybe nine when Jen did it?"

"Jen?" The name pulled at something inside Ally. She turned to look at the barista.

"Yeah. The artist." He nodded toward the picture of a pregnant woman with a star in her tummy. "She died a few years back—we're lucky we have this wall of hers."

"It's beautiful," Ally said honestly, looking at the pictures with more curiosity now. "She was really talented."

"Yeah." A bell sounded, and he looked over his shoulder, to the counter where a couple was waiting to order. "I'd better get back."

She nodded. "Thanks for the coffee."

With one last glance over her shoulder, she slipped out of the diner. Instead of getting back in her car, she turned left and began to walk down the street, toward the soft sound of gently rolling waves.

Ally had never even flirted with the idea of leaving the city. She loved the hustle and bustle of traffic, people, busyness, and restaurants spilling out onto the sidewalk, performers on the street corner. She liked the anonymity that came of being in a crowd. Small towns weren't like that, and Cape Hope definitely wasn't.

Since arriving in town a few days ago, she'd been completely embraced by these people—not treated with suspicion as she might have expected. Everyone had been so kind, despite the fact she was an outsider.

As for the town itself, she hadn't really been prepared to find it beautiful, and yet she did. She walked down the street, studying the timber shop fronts, old and weathered, some in need of paint, but all so charming and quaint. One building in particular stood out—a beautiful old art deco movie theater. The building itself was cream, with turquoise and red details, gold as well, the windows painted in an ornate scrawl that proudly proclaimed the titles of old films. She slowed her pace without realizing it, fascinated by the cinema, imagining how many people had enjoyed evenings there over the years. Closer inspection made Ally wonder if the cinema had been closed for quite some time—it had an air of disuse about it. A sign, which read The Regency, was largely obstructed by an opportunistic ivy vine, scrambling hungrily over the roof and down the front of the building.

Thinking what a shame it was that a building of such beauty should pass its point of usefulness to the town, Ally kept walking, scanning the streetscape, noting things she'd missed the first few times she'd driven through town.

There were neat potted plants in front of many of the little shops, all carefully tended, and despite the cold snap, the plants had apparently been chosen for this weather—they were green, despite the chill. Benches were set up out in front of the barber shop and the post office, in case a shopper needed to sit and rest, and as she got nearer to the ocean, the street opened up to parks on both sides.

She chose one, walking across the grass until she crested a gentle hill and the ocean came fully into view. She stopped walking, just so she could stare at it, drinking in the sight of the Atlantic, which seemed to stretch forever, and the pretty pier that danced at its edges.

It was like something out of an old war movie.

Timber, rickety, with a big building on the end that she

imagined would come alive in summer—kids jumping off the edges, ice cream being sold by the cone.

It was really, really lovely, and despite her long-held certainty that city living was the only living, Ally could imagine being very happy if she'd been born in a place like this. Maybe it wouldn't have even left such a huge void in her life when her father had left or her mother had died, if she'd had this kind of community to rally around her.

She pushed the thoughts aside, not willing to go down the road of "what if" and "if only." There was no sense in that.

She had just resumed her path toward the ocean when her phone started to buzz. She lifted it out of her pocket, swiping it to answer when she saw an unfamiliar number. "Hello?"

"Amy." Luke Miller's voice was even deeper and huskier over the phone—without his looks to distract her. Her stomach lurched in response to not just his voice, but also the rush of guilt that accompanied his use of her fake name. She got why she was doing this, but an irrational desire to tell him the truth clipped at her heels. She didn't want him to call her Amy. She wanted to be Ally to him.

"Oh, hey." She winced—could she sound any more like an excitable teenager?

"I've got what I needed to finish the ceiling repairs. Are you at the cottage?"

She ran her eyes over the Atlantic. "No. But I can be."

A pause. "You don't need to rush back. I can get a key from Izzie."

Disappointment burst through Ally and she realized, for the first time, that she was in serious trouble. Because no way on earth was she going to miss a chance to see him again. "No, that's fine. I was literally on my way back. I just wanted to grab a coffee from the diner."

"Okay. See you in an hour?"

A smile stretched her lips and her pulse began to race. "Yeah, okay. An hour."

SHE HADN'T REALLY planned on making lunch. But as she walked back to her car, she passed a market stall set up with displays out the front—old wheelbarrows filled with produce. She couldn't resist grabbing some of the earthiest-smelling beets she'd seen in a long time, and before she knew it she was filling her canvas bag with yams, sprouts, cauliflower, rutabaga, and every seasonal vegetable she could find.

She'd gravitated toward cooking as a career for many reasons. It was what she loved, what she was good at, and it never failed to bring her comfort.

It had been at least a week since she'd made more than toast or eggs, and suddenly she was itching to cook something. It had nothing to do with the fact Luke Miller was due in her house. She just wanted to go back to basics.

She got home before him and set about rinsing, chopping, and sautéing, pleased at how functional the kitchen was for a holiday rental.

When Luke knocked on the door a short time later, the whole of Cardinal Cottage was fragrant with the smell of a thick, hearty soup.

Ally pulled the door open, her eyes moving over him before she could stop herself. "Hi." It was breathless.

"Hi." He stayed exactly where he was, his own gaze chasing the features of her face until she felt completely giddy.

"Come in."

Neither of them moved for several seconds, and then he nodded. "You've been cooking?"

"Oh, yeah." And as soon as she said it, she knew the whole reason for the soup was this. Him. "Have you had lunch?"

"What's lunch?" He grinned.

"You know, that meal between breakfast and dinner."

"Oh, yeah, I've heard about it." He shrugged. "I'm usually too busy to stop."

"Well, I've made a big batch of soup."

"It smells good."

"Thanks. I couldn't resist—there were some incredible vegetables at the market store."

"I thought vegetables came from the frozen section of the supermarket?"

Ally pretended shock. "You're not serious?"

He laughed. "Hey, if it weren't for those little bags, Stella'd never eat anything green."

"But the range at the market's *so* good."

"Yeah, but you have to know what to do with it," he countered. "And I do not."

"You don't cook?"

"I do," he contradicted, placing his bag on a chair at the table, moving toward the soup pot. "But it never smells like this."

Pleasure warmed Ally from the inside. "I have a definite advantage, being a chef and all."

"You're a chef?"

"Yeah." She smiled, self-consciously reaching for her ponytail and pulling it over her shoulder, toying with the ends.

"I'm in awe, Amy." More guilt. It rushed through her, filling her with a blinding sense of panic, so her breath strained in her lungs. He continued, apparently oblivious. "I don't think I could cook a palatable meal to save my life. As Stella takes delight in telling me daily."

Ally lifted her face in time to catch a lopsided smile that punched her right in the gut. He was way too handsome. A sexy single dad with a lopsided grin. Oh, boy. "Summer's okay—we can live on cookouts. But even then, I think she probably needs more than hamburger patties in her diet."

Ally's smile was spontaneous and broad. "You know, cooking's not that hard."

"Says you, the chef." He grinned, reaching over and playfully tapping her arm. It was just a simple gesture, a friendly action, but the second they connected, the air between them hummed and thickened so she was conscious of every single cell in her body.

"I mean it." She turned to the soup, needing a distraction, lifting the lid off and stirring it. "It's not rocket science."

"I don't know. I follow recipes and they just…don't work."

Ally laughed. "You can't be following them properly then."

"I am, I promise." He lifted his hands in the gesture of "Scout's honor."

"Maybe you're not a recipe person, then," she said thoughtfully.

"I think I'm just not a cooking person." He wiggled his brows to show it wasn't something that was keeping him up at night.

"Everyone can learn to cook. You just need a good teacher."

"Are you volunteering, Amy?"

Her breath hitched in her throat as her eyes flew to his, the atmosphere charged with tight awareness. *Ally*, she wanted to correct, but her throat was tight with adrenaline and anticipation. "Do you want to learn?"

He frowned, and she wondered—in the back of her mind, the tiny part of her still capable of any kind of rational thought—if he was feeling this same drugging awareness. "I think it's kind of a matter of life and death," he said with mock seriousness.

She smiled slowly, achingly, the moment burning its way into her soul, his nearness intoxicating and enlivening. "Then it's probably my ethical duty to step up, right?"

He nodded. "Shall we discuss terms over lunch?"

Her laugh was soft, just a slight exhalation. "You've got yourself a deal."

Chapter Six

"SO A CHEF, huh?" he asked as she ladled the thick, fragrant soup into two bowls.

"Yep."

"How'd that happen?"

"I've always been good at cooking. My dad and I used to make pancakes on weekends." She frowned. "Not every weekend." *Not when he was hungover*, she tacked on inwardly. "A few times." Her shrug was awkward. "And it stuck with me. I learned to cook with him, and I guess I just really loved it."

"So you've always known it's what you wanted to do?"

"I guess so." She carried the bowls to the table, warmed when she saw he'd grabbed soup spoons and napkins without her realizing it. He also didn't sit until she was seated, and she gave him a silent tick for his good old-fashioned manners.

"Do you still cook together?"

Ally felt like the world had tipped off its axis. She was hot and cold, panicking again, back in the diner, steeling herself to speak to him, looking for him, knowing her dad was here and he had no idea she'd tracked him down.

She shook her head, concentrating on the soup, moving her spoon through the bowl. It took a second for her to rally her voice. "He...moved out. When I was a kid. I haven't...seen him in a long time."

She lifted her focus to Luke's kind face, and her heart thumped. Again, she felt the weirdest pull to tell him the truth, to explain why she was in Cape Hope. To pour her heart out to him.

It was stupid. Too risky. Self-indulgent. She didn't want to confide in him. She hardly even knew him.

"I'm sorry. They divorced?"

"Yeah, eventually. I mean, he just disappeared, we never saw him again. The divorce was all through lawyers and stuff."

"Jeez."

"Yeah."

She liked that he didn't offer any of the platitudes she'd heard over the years. He just sat there in silence, eating his soup appreciatively, his eyes hooking to hers every few moments, so she felt like he was saying so much, even without using words.

"I don't know if that's it, anyway," he said.

Neither of them had spoken for a long time. She wasn't sure what he meant.

She lifted a brow, waiting.

He'd finished his soup and sat back in his chair, kicking

his legs out in front of him beneath the table so they accidentally brushed her ankles. She shifted, her pulse firing. "My mom loves to cook. I grew up the same as you, helping in the kitchen, watching, learning. It all went in one ear and out the other."

Ally toyed with her ponytail. "I guess you just weren't into it."

"I like food," he said honestly.

"Well, that's a point in your favor. I can never understand people who don't love to eat."

He grinned. "Do they exist?"

"Oh, yeah. I have a friend who will regularly skip dinner if she's been into the restaurant for lunch. I get it—you're not necessarily going to be hungry a few hours after a three-course meal, but it's a wasted opportunity for flavor."

He laughed. "You're a hedonist."

"I guess I am, just a little bit."

"So you're just having a break? Looking for this guy your mom used to know and then heading back to Wisconsin?"

There was a pause. She frowned, the words forming in her mouth, so she had to clamp her lips together to stop from speaking them. *He's not just "this guy." He's my dad and I've found him.* She hadn't told anyone why she was leaving Wisconsin. She hadn't discussed it with another soul. Was that out of a sense of obligation to her mom, who would've been dead set against this? Or was it out of a silly superstitious desire not to jinx herself?

Luke was the first person she'd felt a compulsion to confide in, but she knew it would be silly. And potentially damaging to her plan to surprise—ambush?—her father with her appearance.

"I…" But surely she could trust him? She looked into his eyes and a flash of goodwill filled her soul. Yeah, she could trust him. Probably. Still, she shook her head to clear the direction of her thoughts. It was easier just to answer his question and not be drawn on details as to her mother's "friend." "Yeah. Back to Wisconsin."

"How long do you think you'll be in town for?" It was a simple enough question but she felt like he was looking at her with a layer of intensity that belied such a simple query.

"I'll go back in a couple of weeks, for Christmas," she said quietly, the idea filling her with dread. One lonely Thanksgiving had been bad enough; she couldn't imagine what Christmas Day without her mom would be like.

"I guess you're due back at work?"

She thought about that. "I mean, my job is there if I want it. I know they'd take me back. But, after Mom died, I just wanted to clear my head a bit." She spooned some more soup into her mouth, and they were quiet a moment. "There was a lot to do, packing up her house and arranging for the sale." Emotions shimmered inside of her. "I thought I was doing okay, you know? It's been six months. But, the closer we get to Christmas, the harder it is again. All these memories keep flooding me when I least expect it. Mom loved

Christmas, and she did it so, so well." A nostalgic smile touched Ally's lips. "This year, when the decorations started to go up in shop windows, I just had to get away. I needed to breathe and think. To escape." It was an honest admission, and her eyes clouded over briefly with the depth of her grief.

He was still silent and she liked his quiet contemplation. Finally, though, he leaned forward, propping his elbows on the table, his fingers laced together beneath his chin. "What kinds of things would she do? At Christmas?"

Ally's faint smile was instinctive. "Oh, you know, everything. We had at least two trees, one in the living room and one in the hall, and she'd decorate the whole way down the stairs. We cooked—everything. Puddings, cakes, pies, cookies galore, the works. Gingerbread was our specialty, and we'd make these elaborate houses—more and more so every year—and gift them to our neighbors." Her sigh was just a soft exhalation. "Mom was big on the giving. Even as a kid, it wasn't really about receiving presents so much as doing our part. We'd serve in the soup kitchen at our church on Christmas Eve, and there was usually just a small gift for me on Christmas morning. But it was always the best day of my life."

"That sounds pretty perfect."

"Yeah." Her smile was twisty. "I thought so."

More contemplative silence. "I sometimes wonder I don't do enough of that stuff with Stella."

Ally nodded thoughtfully. "It's got to be hard, as a single

parent."

He expelled a breath and nodded. "It is. And Stella's going through a phase right now. She's pushing all my buttons, all the time. She's a really good kid, but she's…challenging."

Ally frowned, trying to reconcile this account with the little girl she'd met. "How so?"

"Just an attitude and a half. She talks to me like we're equals."

Ally laughed sympathetically. "I guess because it's just the two of you maybe she does feel that? Like she's part of a team, rather than a subordinate." She pondered the idea. "I know I felt that with Mom. I did a lot more around the house to help out than my friends did, and she relied on me more heavily. We were in it together."

"Maybe that's partly it," he agreed cautiously, then shook his head, that same adorable lopsided grin transforming his face. "I'd better get going on this ceiling or it'll never get patched."

Disappointment flashed in Ally's gut. She didn't want their lunch to end, but he'd finished his own soup ages ago and her bowl was empty now, too. "Okay."

She resisted the urge to watch him work. Quickly putting the soup into a Tupperware and storing it in the fridge, she left the pot and bowls in the sink and scooted into the living room to pretend she was reading. But her nerves were jangling hard and fast inside of her.

It turned out patching a ceiling wasn't a quick job. Not

when the leak had spread so far through the drywall. An hour or so after they'd finished lunch, she felt herself being drawn back to the kitchen and finally gave in to temptation, padding through the house to stand in the door frame.

And heat spread through her body, awareness filling her, because there was no ignoring the way he made her feel. She didn't *want* to ignore it.

She stood there and stared at him, noting everything she could, from the strength of his bearing to the way his denims hugged his rear, to the depth of his tan that spoke of a lot of time outdoors, the thick head of hair her fingers tingled to lift up and grab. She stared at him in a way that made no sense but that she was powerless to stop—until he shifted and caught a glimpse of her in his peripheral vision, straightening on the stepladder so he could look at her properly.

She didn't move. She couldn't. She stared up at him, her heart pumping way too hard, flooding blood through her body so fast it was like being caught up in a tidal wave of feeling. "I…just wanted…to see…" The words wouldn't form; her mouth was dry.

He continued to stare down at her, not moving, not speaking, just a muscle throbbing at the base of his jaw that intrigued and fascinated her.

She cleared her throat, blinking, trying to calm her frantic pulse. "Do you think you'll be much longer?"

He was quiet for a moment, still looking at her thoughtfully, before he began to climb down the stepladder, wiping his hands on the front of his jeans. "Do you need to head out?"

"No."

"It's probably another hour's work."

"Okay." She spun away, moving too quickly and banging her shoulder on the doorjamb as she went. She winced, lifting a hand to it, the pain sharp.

"Hey." He was right behind her, his broad hands on her forearms, stilling her. "You okay?"

"Yeah." Her lungs were useless. Moving but not taking in enough air. She stared up at him, and all she could think of was how nice his lips were and what they would feel like on hers. "Just clumsy."

He nodded, not moving, and she held her breath—why bother helping her lungs when they'd decided not to help her? When he frowned, his brows knit together and his face was fascinatingly stern. Her fingertips tingled with the same temptation that had made her want to touch his hair, now commanding her to lift up and touch his face, to run across his stubbled cheek.

She didn't.

She couldn't.

Oh, she wanted to, but she was shy and nervous and had no idea if she was misreading everything. So she waited and she hoped, and then he stepped back, a tight smile on his face as he spun toward the kitchen.

"I'll be out of your hair soon."

She frowned, staying where she was a few seconds longer before retreating to the privacy of the living room to mull over what the heck had just happened.

And more importantly, what was happening to her.

A year ago, her life had been just how she'd planned it. Working, loving her job, same friends she'd known all her life, catching up with her mom for regular dinners and lunches. Now? She was completely alone on the other side of the country with an all-consuming, fast-developing crush on exactly the kind of man she should run a mile from.

Ally didn't do commitment. She didn't do serious, and everything about Luke Miller screamed serious. It wasn't just the fact that he had a daughter, though that was a part of it. It was *him.* He had this wise-beyond-his-years thing going on, and even talking to him made her feel like she was in way over her head.

She did some reading, or tried to, while she waited for him to finish up. When he came into the living room a little while later, she pretended not to notice. It was childish, but she felt completely off balance.

"That's all done," he said. "It'll need to dry out completely, but I can come back in a week or so to do the painting."

"Okay, great." She swallowed, her mouth dry.

His eyes were appraising as they studied hers. "You're sure you really want to waste your holiday teaching this cooking newbie his way around the kitchen?" He was giving her an out.

She didn't want it. "I'm looking forward to it."

She stopped just a foot or so short of him. She'd heard people talk about chemistry, had read about it in romance novels, but she'd never understood the reality of it; she hadn't known it was a palpable, appreciable reaction some people were capable of sparking off each other. Up close to him like this, she *felt* the air between them change, like her veins had been hooked up to live wires, and she was operating on a different frequency.

"How's Friday?"

She swallowed. "Friday?"

"Stella's at a sleepover. You could come 'round and show me the ropes."

Anticipation spun inside of her. "Sure." Her nod was a quick acceptance. "Friday. That sounds good."

"Yeah."

He didn't move.

Neither did she.

"Is there…" Her voice was so quiet. She cleared her throat. "Anything in particular you want to learn to cook?"

He let out a soft sound, his body still close to hers. "Something I can manage. I'm not exaggerating. I have pretty much zero skills. I could melt pasta."

He was warm. She imagined leaning closer, brushing her body to his, feeling his hardness and strength against her own soft contours. Desire made her voice breathy. "How about we start with a roast chicken?"

"Really? I feel like that's way above my pay grade."

"People always think it's complicated, but actually, it's one of the easiest things you can do and the leftovers will keep you going for days." Memories lifted her lips into a small smile. "I mastered a perfect roast chicken when I was eight years old. I'm sure a guy who can raise a child and fix a hole in the ceiling will be able to cope with basting a bird."

He let out a low whistle. "That sounds like a challenge."

"It is." She wiggled her brows teasingly.

"Damn it. I've never said no to a challenge." He winked, and her breath was burning again, her lungs failing to inflate properly. His eyes bore into hers for several seconds then dropped to her lips and her mouth opened on a husky, hopeful exhalation.

She swayed forward a little, so close she could feel his warmth. "I…" She had no idea what she was going to say. She stood there, so close there was only a breath between them, her eyes locked to his, her knees weak and wobbly.

"You…?" he prompted, and just for a moment, for the briefest of seconds, his hand brushed hers. A groan balled in the pit of her stomach. She stared up at him, completely lost.

She couldn't think of what she wanted to say. She was drowning in his proximity.

"So I'll see you Friday?" His question was gruff, a frown on his face showing he was as confused by this as she was.

"Friday. Yeah." She nodded, not moving.

"Around eight?"

She swallowed and, right when she was thinking of moving a tiny bit closer, so they were properly touching, he blinked hard, like he was waking up from a dream, and stepped backward. Disappointment was a physical pain in her gut. "Eight's fine."

He grinned, lifting a hand to his forehead, tilting an imaginary cap, as though that insanely distracting moment had never happened. "See you then, ma'am." At the door, he turned back to face her, and Ally was right where she'd been a moment ago. "What shall I pick up?"

She furrowed her brow. "Don't shop. I'm scared you'll get everything out of the freezer section."

He grinned. "I'm more self-sufficient than I look, you know."

"You look plenty self-sufficient." The words were out before she could stop them, and she lifted a hand to cover her mouth as her cheeks bloomed hot. He laughed, shaking his head a little, and mortification made her toes curl.

"I really appreciate this," he said gently, letting her off the hook.

She nodded, wanting him to go—immediately before she embarrassed herself more.

"See you Friday."

"Uh-huh." Once he'd closed the door, she swept her eyes shut and rocked onto her heels. *Girl, you are one big-mouthed fool.*

She stayed on the spot until she heard his pickup drive away, then she moved into the kitchen on autopilot in search of a coffee.

And nearly sighed, because Luke Miller had patched the roof, cleaned up after himself and done their lunch dishes. She moved toward the sink, smiling to herself, to see the soup pot and their bowls all stacked neatly on the rack.

There was a note, too.

I'm really glad you came to Cape Hope. LM.

LEAVING THE NOTE had been kind of stupid.

Hadn't he spent pretty much every moment since he met Amy telling himself he needed to fight whatever this crazy connection was between them? Hadn't he spent almost the whole time reminding himself that he wasn't interested in any kind of relationship, especially not with a woman who'd blown into town, basically on a whim, and who'd told him she planned to go away again just as quickly?

He couldn't do that. Not to himself, not to Stella. Not to Amy, either.

Because he felt some kind of vulnerability in her that made all his masculine Marine Corp tendencies zip to the fore. He wanted to protect her, and she didn't particularly seem to want protecting. He wanted to keep her safe and make her happy, and he'd promised himself he wouldn't get caught up in any of that. If things had been different…

But he already had a Number One girl in his life. There wasn't room for another.

AS IT TURNED out, knowing she was going to Luke's house to cook dinner meant she tossed and turned all night.

She gave up on trying to sleep before dawn and went for a run instead, tracking along the creek until it got close to the ocean and then doubling back. She paused a little way from the cottage, hands on her hips, staring up at the wintry blue sky she could see through the spindly trees. A red-breasted robin watched her, his chest proudly puffed out, his dark, intelligent eyes glistening, reminding her of Luke's eyes in a way that made no sense. She began to run again, but memories of Luke's eyes chased her, so she found she was short of breath for reasons other than the exertion.

If she wasn't careful, Luke Miller could complicate everything. She was already spending way too much time thinking about him, wondering about him, when she was in Cape Hope for one reason only.

The smile on her face slipped. Her father's face filled her mind, and she closed her eyes for a second, slowing her pace as the reality of what she was doing threatened to overwhelm her.

Her mother would have hated that Ally was here in Cape

Hope, that she was looking for her dad, that she'd actually found him, after all this time.

"He's not worth another thought, Ally. He walked out on us. Forget he exists."

That had been her refrain, any time Ally had wondered aloud about him.

Forget he exists.

The problem was, that was much easier said than done. Especially now he was within reach. It was as though the thread between them had strengthened, just with that one quick sighting, and she couldn't cut it again.

She wasn't sure she could forgive her dad—maybe she never would. Lord knew she'd spent the better part of her teens hating him with all her soul. It was highly likely that feeling would be with her until the day she died.

She might walk away from this whole thing still hating him, or maybe she wouldn't. Just maybe there was something he could say that would make everything better. Maybe he'd have an excuse, a reason, and suddenly the black pit of worthlessness that lived in her chest would recede until it was gone altogether.

Yeah, and look at those pigs flying past her window. The cottage came into sight. She slowed a little, reaching for a leaf as she ran under a branch, pulling it loose and toying with it between her fingers. She held it as she shouldered her way into the door, then placed it on the hallstand. A frown remained in place as she jogged up the stairs.

She'd thought about her father a lot over the years, specifically about his reasons for leaving without a trace. She'd talked to her mom about it. Dr. Hollis. She couldn't come up with a single reason that could justify his leaving. And especially not his staying away.

Missing out on her graduation. Her prom. The time she'd broken her arm and everyone she knew signed her cast. Her piano recitals. She swallowed hard, pulling off her jogging gear before heading into the shower.

She'd waited a long time for answers. It was time to get them—time to confront her father.

She tried to act like it was "business as usual" as she drove into Beauty Falls, listening to her usual songs, taking comfort from their resonance with her old life, the lyrics flowing through her like a current. Music could do that—hold a mirror up to your soul and capture a slice of it. She couldn't hear "Wrecking Ball" without thinking of her graduation year, and the way she'd felt like she was standing on the precipice of a whole new life. She felt like that again now, her tummy doing loop-the-loops, anxiety and adrenaline pushing through her, pumping her blood fast and loud.

She pulled into a parking spot, grabbing her trench coat and scarf from the passenger seat and bundling up as she climbed out. The temperature had dropped overnight; when she breathed in, she felt ice in the air.

"Morning." She turned around, a friendly local smiling at her.

Caught off guard, her city instincts kicking in, it took a second to lift her own smile into place. "Hey."

"Cold one, eh?"

"Icy," she agreed, locking her car and tossing a smile over her shoulder as she headed toward the café.

It was warm and busy inside, and classical music played—her favorite Erik Satie song that carried far different memories from Miley Cyrus.

"It's a sad song, Daddy."

"Is it, pumpkin? Why do you say that?"

"It's slow and...it makes me sad."

He smiled. "I think it's ethereal."

"What does that mean?"

"It makes you think about what's out there. Bigger things. Beyond us, and this life."

"Like Nana?" she prompted, thinking of the beloved grandmother they'd lost two years earlier.

"Kind of."

"Hey, it's you again." The waitress—Benita's—face came into view, youthful and exuberant, and Ally blinked, pushing memories of her dad and their shared love, not just of cooking, but also of classical music, deep down inside of her.

He'd been wrong.

This was a sad song. Beautiful, too, but ultimately sad, and she let it wash over her for a moment before nodding. "Yeah, hi. Good morning."

"It's a foul morning," Benita contradicted with a rueful smile. "But that's the way it is around here at this time of year. Come on in, grab a table. Let me get you a cup of coffee."

Ally nodded distractedly, taking the same seat she'd occupied the other day. Her dad was already at the window, placing a couple of plates on the counter. A wave of relief that he was here surged through her, but it was followed immediately by nausea. Disbelief. Doubt.

She watched, noting more details this time—a ring on his middle finger, thick and shining silver, a black leather band around one wrist, deep lines on his face. The fact he had a suntan despite it being the middle of winter—she looked down at her own slender arms, golden just like his, and the sting of his betrayal snaked through her anew.

"Anything to eat today?"

Ally turned her attention to Benita as she placed a mug of coffee on the table. Her smile was difficult to muster. "Just a coffee."

"You staying in town?"

"No." Ally swallowed. "I'm over in Cape Hope."

"What brings you to Beauty Falls so often?"

"People around here ask a lot of questions," she muttered, forgetting for a moment that she was meant to be a carefree tourist.

Benita laughed. "Yep. Surely do. There's no secrets in this part of the world."

Ally's heart pirouetted inside of her in perfect timing with the last movement of the Satie song.

Benita propped her pen behind her ear and tapped a manicured nail against the notepad she wrote orders on. "I feel like I know you from somewhere."

Ally's lungs felt weak. "I've only been in North Carolina a week."

"Never visited before?"

"Nope." Ally shook her head, plastering a wistful look on her face. "You must be thinking of someone else."

"Must be," Benita agreed. "Okay, I'll grab your coffee." She turned and cut through the restaurant, moving past the window on her way to the coffee machine.

Her father was there. He smiled as Benita passed, and Ally felt like she'd been kicked in the guts. Because if she didn't know anything about him, she'd have said he was a nice, normal, happy, well-adjusted guy. He was handsome and well-dressed. There was nothing in his bearing to say he was the kind of man who could desert his family—who could disappear into thin air.

Why hadn't he cared enough to stay? Or at least stay in contact? He'd fallen completely out of her life, walking away from her like she meant nothing.

Like her mom meant nothing.

"Food's up."

Without warning, his eyes shifted to Ally's, and everything stopped, completely still. The world stopped spinning, the air stopped moving, the noise ceased so it was deathly silent. Everything stopped. There was nothing and no one there, just Ally and her dad. This was it—the moment. The moment she now recognized she'd spent all her life waiting for.

As a teenager, she'd lain awake nights imagining what she'd say if she came face-to-face with her dad again, how she'd punish him for leaving her, what perfectly shaped insult she'd throw at his feet. Or would she throw herself into his arms and bury her head against his chest and simply breathe him in, remembering the way he'd held her tight as a kid, remembering how for a short time in her life he'd been the one person who could make her feel like everything was going to be okay?

Sitting only six or so feet away from the man who'd broken her heart beyond repair, all she could do was stare at him. No words came to her, no anger, no sadness, just silent, desperate confusion and a feeling that maybe if she looked for long enough she'd begin to fathom all of this.

"Here you go." Benita appeared at Ally's side, placing the coffee down, and Ally startled. The world began to spin, noise burst through her—too loud, too bright—so she winced a little, struggling to bring herself back to the diner and to remember where she was and why.

She blinked and the moment shifted away from her. Jack Monroe moved, clearly not recognizing her, deeper into his kitchen, away from her view.

She'd always wondered about this. If she were to see her dad again, somewhere random, like passing each other on a busy street, would they know each other? It had kept her awake nights, worrying that she might run into him and not know. She'd wondered if he'd look like she remembered and if he'd be able to pick the relics from her face of the six-year-old she'd been, even now as a woman of twenty-six.

Now she had her answer. She'd sat across a crowded café from her dad and had looked into his eyes and seen nothing. Not even a hint of recognition.

He didn't know her. He didn't remember her. He didn't love her.

And despite the fact she'd come to the café determined to talk to him, determined that she'd get this confrontation over with and tell him who she was and what she thought of him, panic and anxiety drilled through her, so all she wanted was to be alone again. Alone like she probably always would be. She bowed her head to disguise the fact her eyes were moist, staring at the complicated wood grain of the café's tabletop.

The people who matter show up. It was another of her mother's pieces of wisdom. Sasha Monroe had said it often. When Ally had assured her mom she didn't need to come watch her debates, she'd been insistent. Despite the fact she'd worked long hours, she hadn't missed any of the important milestones in Ally's life.

Once, she'd heard her mother explaining to a friend that she was both Ally's mom and dad, and that meant she had to be there twice as much. At the time, Ally had instinctively rejected the sentiment, bristling against what she'd taken to be an assault on her independence. But now her heart swelled with love and appreciation for the mom who'd loved her so damned much she'd been determined Ally would never feel the absence of her father.

If only she'd understood that no one could make up for a dad who decided not to be in her life. Her mom's efforts had been noble and self-sacrificing, but ultimately futile.

Ally hadn't gone a single day without thinking of her dad.

Had he thought of her?

A lump thickened in her throat.

You are the best thing I've ever done, baby.

Those were the words Sasha had spoken at her last birthday. She'd reached over and put her hand over Ally's, and Ally had laughed because it wasn't like her mom to be so sentimental.

A few months later, a massive heart attack had robbed Ally of her mom. And so, what? She'd come to find her dad? As though her mom could be so easily replaced? As though her dad deserved a chance to know her? As though in dying, Sasha's wishes could be forgotten?

A sense of disloyalty and self-disgust swamped Ally. She could hardly breathe. Her mom would hate this, and suddenly, Ally hated it, too. She hated that she'd come, hated that she was sitting here in the same place as the dad who'd run out on her, hated that she thought she could go up to him and tell him who she was.

Her feelings were a tangle inside of her, knotty and indecipherable. But her legs were itching to run, to take her away from here, away from this, to run so hard and fast she escaped her thoughts and memories.

She needed to get away suddenly. She was drowning, and this café was like a riptide, pulling her too fast, too deep.

She drank her coffee so quickly it scalded her tongue a little, left a tip, and slipped out of the restaurant before she could see him again. Ally cried the whole way back to Cape Hope.

Chapter Seven

HE'D BEEN SINGLE for a long time. It was natural that dating would feel weird. Was this a date? It sure felt like it. Jeez. He was actually nervous.

Nervous!

Him, Luke Miller. He'd been to war, he'd faced down IEDs, sniper rifles, death. He'd lost the woman he loved with no warning. He was a single dad.

To Stella.

He was tougher than steel boots. So why had he spent the better part of the last three hours going over the kitchen with a fine-tooth comb?

Because he cared what she thought. He cared what Amy thought more than he liked to admit, even to himself, but the last few hours had forced him to admit he was in way over his head.

With a rueful grimace, he put on a playlist—country guitar—and grabbed a beer from the fridge. He was being ridiculous.

It wasn't a date. It was just a neighbor helping a neighbor out. Just like always happened in this neck of the woods.

He grabbed his guitar off the wall and sat on the edge of the coffee table, strumming along with the music, pausing now and again to have a drink from his beer.

It took four songs for Amy to arrive.

Headlights came up the drive, sweeping around toward his house, and Luke stood, putting the guitar back in its stand as though apprehension wasn't hammering his insides. As though everything was completely normal.

She'd just stepped out of her car when he got to the porch, and his gut did that weird squishy squeeze thing he was starting to get used to whenever he saw Amy. It was a frigidly cold night, and she was dressed accordingly—a trench coat, scarf, hood pulled up.

"Hey." She smiled at him slowly, shyly, but there was something else, a weariness in her face that had him frowning.

Concern filled him. "Hey yourself. You okay?"

She blinked, looking to pull herself together. "Yeah." Her smile was overbright, though. She came around to the rear of the car and popped the trunk, pulling out a brown paper grocer's bag. He reached for it on autopilot, taking it from her arms. The gesture brought them closer together, and he felt an overriding impulse to kiss her cheek.

If this were a normal date, he'd have done that. He'd have kept the groceries in one arm, like he had them now, and put the other low around her waist, holding her close to his side.

But it wasn't a date.

It wasn't a date.

Her eyes cast over his house and that weird, dippy sense of nervousness was back, as though her liking his home was the most important thing in his universe.

"This is nice," she murmured softly, flicking her eyes to his.

Pleasure burst in his gut. "Thanks."

"Have you lived here long?"

"Yeah." He nodded. "Since I was sixteen." He opened the door for her, and the light from the hallway showed him her face better.

She was so beautiful, but it was more than that. She fascinated him. He liked looking at her, watching her, seeing how she felt through those expressive eyes, eyes that he felt he could look at for a ridiculous amount of time.

She stepped inside, and he followed.

"My pops needed the company. After Nana died, he struggled to keep up with the place, and I wasn't on great terms with Mom and Dad. Everyone agreed it'd be better if I moved here for a while. Help him out, give Mom and Dad a bit of a break." He grimaced, shaking his head.

"Were you some kind of delinquent, Luke?" she teased, and she was more like herself with every second that passed. Relief flowed through him. He liked her like this. Playful. Happy. Teasing. Then she shrugged out of her trench and scarf, draping them over the hat stand, and he had to use all his energy not to let his gaze wander down her body.

It's not a date. It's not a date.

He didn't date, and she was just visiting Cape Hope.

"I was *borderline* delinquent," he confessed, grinning, gesturing for her to move deeper into the house.

"I find that hard to believe."

"It's true. It's one of the reasons I enlisted. I think if I hadn't found the Marines, I'd probably have gone off the rails."

"You?" She dragged her eyes over his body, and his gut clenched, desire—unmistakable desire—supercharging his blood.

"Yeah, me." His voice was deeper than usual, even to his own ears.

She arched a brow skeptically. "So the Marines saved you?"

"Something like that."

She strolled ahead of him, her gaze chasing the details of the room in a way that only exacerbated his earlier hope that she like his place.

His home.

He watched as she moved around the living room, looking at pictures on the walls—baby photos of Stella, his wedding photo with Jen, a family photo with his mom and dad, Nana and Pops. His high school graduation, one of him in his military blues. She paused a little at that one, giving it an extra good look, then moved to the guitar stand.

"You play?" she asked.

"Yeah." His voice came out gruff. He smiled. "Just about since I could walk."

Her face swiveled to his, speculation in her eyes, then she returned to looking around. He tried to see the place through her eyes—it was a big, open, two-story farm house, with a wraparound veranda, and this living room was where he and Stella spent most of their time. It had a homey, lived-in feel, and he didn't have much of an eye to decorating. A lot of the pretty stuff was Jen's choice and had probably dated badly.

But he liked it.

"It's really nice," she said, a little wistfully, then cleared her throat. "Where's the kitchen?"

"This way." He expelled a breath he hadn't realized he was holding and led the way into the rustic space. The fittings were all pretty original. Sometime around the fifties the cabinetry had been upgraded, but it was good quality wood and, apart from needing an occasional paint touchup, it hadn't needed much work. *It's retro*, Jen had insisted when he'd suggested replacing it. *I like it.*

So it had stayed, and now, he was used to it.

"This is so charming," she gushed, moving in and running a hand over the thick oak countertop. "A kitchen full of love and memories. Just like they should be."

He was already pretty into her, but hearing Amy describe his house with such insight did something funny in his gut, like he felt bubbles popping or something. He placed the grocery bag on the counter, while Amy moved to the fridge, smiling as she looked over the pictures he'd taped there.

"They're all old," he explained. "When she was little, she loved to draw. I try to encourage her, but she just doesn't have much interest in it anymore. She must get her artistic skills from me."

"I saw the mural, in the diner," Amy said, spinning around to face him, her eyes roaming his face.

Luke smiled. That was a happy memory. "Yeah?"

"Jen was very talented."

"She was." He frowned. "She got a scholarship, you know, to study art in Chicago."

"Yeah?"

"But we got married, and then she was pregnant. It was something she was always going to do, though, once the baby grew up and started school."

She thought about this, not offering any of the platitudes they shared a dislike for, even though her expression clearly showed sympathy. Finally, she said, "Degree or not, she was obviously good at art. And there aren't many better places than Cape Hope to inspire the soul."

He exhaled slowly. "Yeah, she loved it here." He looked around the house. "Jen's home life was different from mine. They didn't have much of anything growing up and lived in a tiny place just off the highway. All she wanted was to make a nice home for us, for our kids."

He saw sympathy on her face and cringed—he'd really tanked the mood. What was wrong with him? Even on a non-date, it was surely poor form to drag someone through the most miserable memories of your life.

"Anyway." He began to lift things out of the bag. "What have we got here?"

She came to stand beside him, watching as he removed things. She was so close he could feel her warmth, and then her hand was on his shoulder. He looked down at her—up close, their height difference was more noticeable—and her eyes were serious. "It's okay to talk about her," she murmured. "And it's okay to feel sad about it."

A muscle jerked in his jaw. He nodded. "I know. It's just…six years, you know?"

"Yeah." Her smile was gentle, understanding. She looked like she was on the brink of saying something, her lips parted, her brow furrowed, so he could practically hear her cogs turning. He waited, and he memorized everything about this, about how close she was, how good her hand felt on his shoulder, how sweet she smelled, how she had a tiny little constellation of freckles dancing across the bridge of her nose, how her eyes were actually blue and green with sparkles of gold. He stared down at her, and she stared back at him, and his head dropped nearer, and he was so close to kissing her before she blinked and stepped back, her expression a little dazed.

"You okay?"

She nodded, but it was jerky, and he remembered the way she'd been when she'd stepped out of the car.

"You sure?"

Another nod, but this time, a little frown crossed her face. "There's something…about you," she said finally, a look of frustration in her features. "Like I want to talk to you."

He laughed softly. "Aren't we talking?"

"I mean, *really* talk to you." She swallowed so the column of her throat shifted visibly and his eyes chased the simple gesture. "I feel like I can tell you stuff."

"What stuff?" he prompted.

She lifted her shoulders, her eyes flared wide, emotions clouding their clarity. "Nothing in particular."

Her frown stayed locked in place for a second and, before he knew what he was doing, Luke found himself lifting a hand to her cheek, running his fingers over her soft flesh, his gut kicking hard. "You can talk to me." The words were graveled, intense.

She swallowed again. He kept his hand where it was, his thumb padding over her skin like it was the most natural thing in the world. He waited, and she was quiet, and he could have sworn anguish shifted in her delicate features. He held his breath, hoping she'd talk to him, wanting her to say whatever was on her mind.

But she blinked and smiled, a smile so bright it almost knocked him completely off course.

"Thanks!" It was too loud. She blinked, shaking her head and stepping away from him. "Where are your chopping boards?"

He reached into the drawer for one, placing it on the counter beside the groceries, but a sense of dissatisfaction was hovering on the periphery of his mind now. Like she really did want to talk to him about something, something that mattered, but for some reason couldn't.

"So the first thing I'm going to do is turn the oven on and get a baking dish ready. You got a tray?"

He pulled one from the oven. He couldn't force her to confide in him. This wasn't a date. They weren't a couple. She was a woman he'd just met who had her own life and her own troubles. All he could do was be there if she wanted to talk. And he'd already offered that.

"Great. Preheat the oven to four-fifty degrees."

He turned the dials while she washed her hands at the sink.

"Perfect. Now, we're going to want to take the bird out of the plastic."

"Really? You don't leave it in?" It was a joke, said with a smile.

She laughed, elbowing him playfully, completely like herself again now, so he could almost believe he'd imagined her earlier sense of pain.

He breathed in; her shampoo was like vanilla. His chest shifted. "I like to do it by the sink," she explained, lifting the chicken and nodding toward the pan. "Because chickens are kind of gross to handle, and I want to wash my hands right after."

"You're a chef and you think they're gross?"

"I'm still a human, and they're all kind of slimy and wet."

He laughed. She had a point.

"So, just grab a sharp knife to split the bag," she explained, cutting it open, then placing it into the pan. "You can also do this on a chopping board, but I figure it's better to contain the mess to one site."

"Right."

"So, remove the giblets bag—"

"Now I'm with you on the 'gross' thing."

"Yeah." She grinned, reaching into the bird.

But he shook his head, putting a hand out and covering her arm. "Hold up. No deal, Amy."

"What?" She looked at him, arm inside the bird's cavity, and he almost laughed at the contradictory feelings that were looping through him—desire warring with amusement.

"You're here to teach, not do. Take a seat and tell me about your day, boss me around. I'm the chef tonight."

She arched a brow. "You think you're up to it, Mr. Can't-Make-Pasta?"

"Thanks for the vote of confidence, but yeah. I got this."

"Okay, if you're sure." Her smile was like lightning. It sparked right inside of him.

"I'm sure."

She pulled her hands away and flicked the kitchen sink on with her elbow—one of the few parts of the place that had been modernized out of necessity, when the water had frozen in the taps a couple of winters ago. He watched as she lathered her hands, washing them thoroughly, and then moved to the barstools and sat down in one.

"Now, ma'am, what'll you have? Wine? Water? Whiskey?"

She pulled a face at the final suggestion. Not a whiskey girl, apparently. "Maybe a beer?"

"Beer, I have." He moved to the fridge and pulled one out, cracking the lid and handing it to her. This time, their fingers touched and neither of them rushed to pull away. She looked up at him and it was like he was drowning or being sucked into the ocean. He didn't—couldn't—do anything to break this contact.

She was beautiful, distractingly so, but there was something else about her. Something familiar and different, fascinating and closed off. He just wanted to stare at her and lose himself in her for hours.

"So." She cleared her throat, smiling a little—an awkward smile, self-conscious and nervous all at once. Her voice was gruff. "Pull the packet out and set it aside. We're going to season the bird first then make the stuffing." She walked him through the next instructions, almost always managing to refrain from laughing, even when he cut the baguette she'd brought into halves and expected it to go in the stuffing like that. "Smaller—like, really fine," she murmured. "Breadcrumbs is more the consistency we're going for. Not sandwich."

He looked at her with a hint of apology. "I should know that. I've only ever seen cubes used."

"Cubes? No way. We're doing this from scratch." She held up her hands, her eyes crinkled at the corners. Jeez, she had a beautiful smile. She smiled with her whole face and it filled his whole body with happiness. "Now, it's just the veggies."

"This is where Stella would do a barf sign," he explained.

"Not at my veggies," she promised.

"I like your confidence."

She lifted her shoulders. "I've fed a lot of kids."

"At your work?"

"Yeah. And at the church Mom and I used to help out at. My mac and cheese is a masterstroke in hidden veggies."

"Mac and cheese? With veggies? That's kind of sacrilegious. Is it still even yellow?"

She nodded with mock seriousness. "Oh, yeah. It's got rutabagas, zucchini, cauliflower, all hidden in a delicious *béchamel* sauce with bacon bits and maple syrup."

"I'm kind of wishing it wasn't already almost nine o'clock. That's making me hungry."

She shot a look at the clock, surprise widening her eyes. "You do realize we're not going to be eating for another hour and a half?"

"I have chips."

"Chips? While we're cooking a chicken? Now who's being sacrilegious?" He arched a brow pleadingly, so she waggled her finger with mock severity. "We will not be ruining our appetite with processed snacks."

"Yes, ma'am." He military saluted, and she relaxed, sipping her beer.

He tried not to think about how good she looked there. How *right* she was in his kitchen. How much he liked seeing her there.

Amy guided him through prepping the vegetables, peeling them, and tossing them in a bowl with olive oil, herbs, and seasoning, then laying them out evenly in the tray, around the chicken. "Now just pop it in the oven."

"I'm not sure this is as easy as you promised."

She rolled her eyes. "You get faster at it. And you can pare it back once you know what you and Stella like. Maybe you'll do fewer vegetables or different seasonings, maybe no stuffing—"

He clutched his hands to his chest, mock wounded. "No stuffing? It's the best part. Well, that and the gravy."

"Oh, and my gravy's really, really good," she promised, and her confidence was another part of her that he found utterly, spellbindingly beautiful.

"So what's your signature dish?"

She tilted her head to the side, thinking about that. "I

love French food. Creamy sauces, garlic, lots of butter. But I usually keep it pretty simple for myself. When you've cooked all day, you don't necessarily want to spend hours in the kitchen. I do lamb chops a lot, and salad. Some grilled chicken." She tilted her head to one side. "Quick and easy. One-pan dishes because I don't like cleaning up."

"Fair enough."

"Where's Stella tonight?"

"She's at a friend's."

"Does she do that often? Stay over?"

"No, it's her first time actually. She's stayed late before and fallen asleep, but I usually go pick her up."

"Not this time?"

"Nah. Marie—my friend's wife—is doing pancakes in the morning, and the girls—their kids—told Stella about it. She wanted to stay."

"And what's that like for you?"

"What do you mean?"

She stood up, moving to the oven, peering through the glass, making sure the chicken was cooking properly. Satisfied, she nodded. "I mean, is it weird not to have her here?"

"Kind of. She does spend time with her uncle—Jen's brother—a fair bit, so it's not like we're always in each other's pockets. But a lot of the time…"

"Are you close to him?"

"Jacob? Yeah. He's like my brother."

"That must be nice, for both of you."

"Jen would like it that we're still tight, that's for sure." He washed his hands and dried them on a towel before picking up his beer and moving back toward the stools, where she'd sat back down again. He propped his hip on the counter beside her, close enough to catch a hint of vanilla. It sent his pulse into overdrive. "So your day? You were going to tell me about it?"

She looked up at him, then away again. Something like consternation crossed her expression and it was as though a light had been turned out. She was withdrawn and quiet, her back tense. So he hadn't been imagining it earlier. "Was I?"

"Yeah."

She bit down on her lip, her brow furrowed, and her change in demeanor had him on high alert. "I went into Beauty Falls."

"Looking for your mom's friend?"

"Yeah."

"And? No luck?"

"Why do you say that?"

"Because you're frowning."

"Am I?"

"No, now you're doing this." He mimicked her surprise, then smiled. "But before, when I asked, you were frowning."

She let out a small, uneven laugh. "You're an expert in reading faces now?"

He nodded sagely. "Sure am."

"I'll have to watch my expressions around you."

He nodded, but he was serious. "I'm sorry you haven't got hold of him yet."

"Yeah." A frown, and again, the strangest sense assailed him that she was trying to tell him more, that she was holding herself back with effort.

"Do you want a hand with it?"

Her eyes jerked to his. "With finding him?"

"Yeah. I mean, I could put some feelers out. Ask around. Jacob might be able to help? He's a cop, knows everyone and everything, and has access to all the county records."

"No." She moved her head from side to side quickly. "No, thanks."

"You're sure? It's no trouble."

"I'll let you know," she said quietly, her lips lifting a little.

This time, her smile didn't change her whole face. This time, it looked a little fake. And he got it. She was shutting him down. End of conversation.

Concern balled inside of him. This wasn't a date, and she wasn't going to be in town long enough for it to become a thing, and still he felt this weird protective surge inside of him, like he wanted to keep her safe and make her happy.

But before he could think of what to say to make it better, Ally spoke. "Come on, why don't you show me the rest of this place?"

Chapter Eight

THEY DIDN'T EAT until almost ten and, by then, Ally had to give Luke extra points for not diving in with his bare hands. He was a big guy and it was *way* past dinnertime.

Instead of going full-blown starved carnivore on her, he held a chair out for her in a way that was so sweet and old-fashioned she had to remind herself that was just his manners, not something special he was doing for her. And yet, even as she told herself that, she thought of the note he'd left, the note she'd stupidly slung into her bag that morning, like it was something she needed with her—a talisman of sorts.

Had it just been a throwaway nicety? A kindness because she'd confided in him about her mom and the loneliness that had driven her out of Wisconsin? Or was there more to it? A promise or something? A hope?

She didn't know, and it was impossible to tell from the way he'd been acting what the heck this dinner was all about.

"So do you need me to write this down?" she asked.

He took the seat opposite her and gestured for her to help herself. He'd opened a wine—a nice bottle, she noted, one even the *sommelier* at her old restaurant would have been impressed by, and that was saying something. "The recipe? I don't think there's a chance in hell I'm going to be able to do this on my own."

She burst out laughing. "Now who's voting no-confidence?"

"I'm just not wired for cooking."

"Anyone can be wired for cooking." She rolled her eyes, then smiled, so a dimple flexed in her cheek. "Maybe this was too much. We'll do pasta next time." As soon as the words *next time* came from her mouth, she knew she'd meant them. She wanted to do this again. She liked being here, cooking with him, standing beside him in the beautifully rustic kitchen, chatting like they were old friends.

"I'm glad I haven't scared you off with my complete lack of knowledge."

"If anything, it's made me more determined."

He watched her appraisingly for so long heat bloomed in her cheeks, and when he answered, it was with a straight face and a voice that was so deep her pulse fluttered wildly at her wrists. "I'm flattered, I guess."

She leaned forward and took a piece of meat for her plate. She added veggies and poured on a little gravy, then sat back and watched him do the same.

Except he kept going and going until there was an impressive amount of food on his plate. He lifted his eyes to hers, saw the speculation there, and laughed a little self-consciously. "Did I mention I'm hungry?"

She grinned. "You did. And I heard your tummy grumble anyway."

If she didn't think it was unlikely for a big, strong country guy like Luke Miller to feel embarrassed, she'd have almost thought he blushed. "I'm usually in bed by now."

"Yeah?"

"Sure."

"You're a morning person?"

He shifted his gaze to the windows, the dark night framed through them. "Only way to be out here."

She ran her tongue over her lower lip, noticing way too much about him in that brief moment when his attention was elsewhere. Like how capable his hands were, how tanned and strong, how interesting his face—handsome, swarthy, and interesting. She thought about how this house was somehow so perfect for him—such a reflection of this man and the life he lived that she felt like being here in his dining room was a bit like seeing inside his heart.

"Plus"—he turned back to her, and she rushed to school her features into a mask of polite attention—"Stella's got to be up for school, so I'm up."

"Right." Ally speared a bean and held it on her fork a moment. "You know, I could teach her a few recipes if you wanted. I loved to cook when I was a kid. I was about her age when my dad left, and I learned to make some meals pretty quick."

"Your mom didn't cook?"

"She did. But she had to start working full-time to keep things going—financially—I mean, he just disappeared, and they didn't have a lot of savings." Anger flared inside of her as she tried to reconcile that man with the man she'd observed at the diner, so calm and smiling, in control. A wave of betrayal made breathing difficult. Hell. What was she doing here? Her mom would be so furious with her.

"That must have been scary for you."

"It was scary." She rushed the words out and tried not to think of her mom, and the pain Ally would be inflicting if she'd lived to see this. "That's a great word for it. As a kid, I guess we want our folks to make things safe and secure and for us to know we have a place in this world. When he left, it just sucked the bottom out of my life, you know?"

"Was it completely out of the blue?" His eyes studied her in a way that was peeling her layers back, piece by piece.

Her voice took on a throaty quality. "The leaving part was, for sure. I mean, they fought all the time. Big fights. He drank a fair bit. As an adult, I kind of look back and can see how miserable they were."

Across the table, Luke frowned.

She reached for her wine, taking a sip. A California Chardonnay, it was buttery and full-flavored, perfect as an accompaniment to the chicken.

"Did he ever make contact?"

Ally thought of the envelope, the mystery as to what had

been inside one that she needed to solve before she could speak about it to anyone else.

"I think he wrote, once or twice."

"You *think*?"

She nodded and, even though she knew it was safer to shut this conversation down, she felt herself being pulled toward him. She felt herself wanting to share some of this burden with someone. No, not just someone. With Luke, specifically. "Mom never forgave him for leaving us. If he wrote me, I didn't get the letters." Luke's brows shot up and the disapproval she felt in his features had her rush to her mom's defense. "He didn't just abandon me," she said with a quiet strength. "Mom was never the same after he left."

He nodded, wiping his hand over his jaw in a gesture she now knew showed that he was in deep thought. He didn't speak, and after a few moments, she filled the silence, memories pricking at her skin so goosebumps dotted her flesh.

"They fought all the time, but it was always fine a day or two later. You know? Kind of like a hurricane. There was the buildup and then the storm and then a few days of absolute devastation while you took stock of things and, then, life picked up its normal pace all over again. When they weren't fighting, they seemed happy enough, apart from his drinking. Mom used to go on about that quite a bit."

"I guess it's natural she wouldn't have liked it."

"Yeah." Ally nodded.

"Did he work?"

"He was a chef."

Luke lifted a thick, dark brow but stayed otherwise silent.

"He lost his job, about six months before he left. Things got even worse after that. I mean, Mom worked, but we never seemed to have enough money."

"What did your mom do for work?"

Ally smiled, these memories pleasanter. "She was a teacher. And a darned good one, too. She loved her kids—lived for them. Our church couldn't hold all the people who came to her memorial, you know. Mourners spilled out onto the streets. She'd taught in our neighborhood for almost thirty years and had no thoughts of retiring. It was her calling."

They sat in contemplative silence a moment, Luke eating appreciatively, Ally watched him without even realizing she was doing it, until he looked up at her and smiled, and her blood began to rush and hum through her body.

"This is really good," he said.

Pleasure warmed her. "I'm glad you like it."

"So you picked up the slack after he left?"

"I guess so. I didn't see it like that at the time. I just wanted to make everything better for Mom."

"You must have been kind of confused."

"Yeah, that's a good word for it." She sipped her wine thoughtfully. "Sad, confused, then angry. So angry." She blinked to clear the thoughts, turning to look at the darkness beyond the window. She could just make out the shapes of the trees against the black sky.

"Are you still angry?"

"Yes," she answered without missing a beat. "But it's a different anger. A calmer feeling, filled with curiosity and questions. The older I've got, the less it made sense. How could a guy just disappear from his family? How could he have walked out on me?"

She bit down on her lip to stop from saying the rest of that sentence: *How could he stop loving his own daughter?* It was a question that hurt too much even to voice.

"I don't know," Luke answered gently. "I can't imagine that. Stella's my life—I could never leave her."

"That's how it should be." She smiled wistfully, and forced a conversation change before she told him the real reason she was in town. But even as she nudged them in a different direction, she wondered if she really needed to keep this secret any longer.

Surely she could trust Luke not to tell anyone? He was just one guy. What if he knew the real purpose for her being here?

And what could she say? *Oh, by the way, I've been lying to you these last few times we've met? And even though I'm sitting in your house surrounded by pictures of your late wife and your daughter, you don't even know my real name?*

Panic flared—a new type of panic—and she shifted away from the trickiness of that situation. "Have you always lived in Cape Hope?"

"All my life." He nodded. "Except for when I was stationed overseas."

"What was your rank?"

"Lance Corporal Miller at your service."

"Sounds fancy. Should I salute or something?"

He grinned. "Do you want to salute?"

Ally banked down on the butterflies rampaging through her system. Suddenly, she wanted to do a *lot* more than salute. She ignored his question, but she couldn't tamp down on its effects. "Where were you stationed?"

"Iraq."

"Wow."

"Wow?"

"Yeah. That must have been…I don't know. I can't imagine. What was it like?"

His face flickered with memories and thoughts. "It's…hard to explain," he said honestly, a grimace of apology on his handsome face. "There are parts of Iraq that are incredibly beautiful. Ancient towns, cities that have stood their place for millennia."

"But you didn't spend a lot of time in those parts?"

"No."

They finished eating in silence. Then, when their plates were empty, he quietly laid his cutlery down, leaned back in his chair, and fixed her with a steady gaze.

His expression was without emotion, and yet she felt it barreling off him in waves. "Iraq was everything you imagine it to be—and then some. Dry, hot, the stench of death everywhere you looked. It was hard, and each day was interminably long, yet there were great friendships formed in those deserts. We had to rely on each other to survive."

She nodded, not having any words she could offer that were fitting of his sacrifice.

"Jen hated it. She hated that I enlisted. She begged me not to go."

"I can imagine," Ally said honestly. She barely knew Luke, and for some reason the idea of him having been in a warzone filled her veins with ice.

"I went anyway." He lifted his wineglass and took a drink, then fixed his gaze on the window. "I told myself that every day I got to wake up was a gift. You don't take anything for granted over there. Not your friends, not your life, nothing. You just get your head down and do your job. I was prepared to die. I expected to die." He turned back to Ally. "I lost friends. Good ones." His hand lifted to the tags at his neck, and her heart lurched for this unconscious gesture of memory and pain. "Nothing prepared me for losing Jen, though."

Silence—poignant and loaded with the seriousness of his words—filled the room, and then his expression shifted, just a minor change, but she felt it, and the mood lifted.

"Let me show you something?" He stood, holding a hand out to her, and Ally hesitated for the smallest second before putting her own in his.

It was just a simple contact, but shard of lightning flashed from the tips of her fingers to the center of her chest. She bent her head to hide the effect, following him from the table. He grabbed a blanket from the back of one of the leather sofas as they went, sliding open the glass door onto the porch.

It was freezing outside—his reason for grabbing the blanket became clear as he dropped her hand and wrapped the wool around her shoulders.

"Thanks." She smiled up at him, so close, so distracting, and her heart jolted.

He smiled in acknowledgment then moved down the porch steps. At the bottom, he turned around and held his hand out once more. It felt so *right*, walking hand in hand with him like this, across the wide grass lawn in front of his place, pausing a little way from the house.

"When I was a kid, I used to come out here and stare up at the stars." He sat down on the grass; she followed suit. "I'd stare up at them and see the shapes, telling myself stories about them."

He was quiet for a few moments. "It's strange, but these stars became some kind of anchor. I used to stand in the desert and look up, and I could almost imagine I was back here again. They were the one thing that felt familiar, the one thing that made me think I was on earth and not in hell."

Ally nodded, her heart kerthunking. It was freezing out.

She grabbed the edge of the blanket and handed it to him, an invitation in her eyes. He took it, pulling the fabric over his own shoulder, so they sat side by side beneath the blanket's warmth. It wasn't like they were stripping naked and jumping into bed, but Ally's heart raced in exactly the same way. She was conscious of everything. The heaviness of his breathing, the raspy quality to his voice, the warmth of his body, his masculine fragrance, his nearness, his strength.

Overhead, a single bright light caught the periphery of Ally's attention. She lifted to look at it, a little gasp of surprise escaping her lips. She didn't see the way Luke's gaze lingered on her face, nor did she notice the way he shifted closer, as though he couldn't help himself.

"Look," she whispered. "A shooting star."

Reluctantly, he followed her gaze. "Make a wish." The words were soft, gentle, and her eyes flew to his, because Ally wasn't sure what she could wish for beyond this moment.

"Do you believe in that?" she asked instead.

He was so close to her. Ally's pulse hammered inside of her and desire sledged through her. "In magic?"

She bit down on her lip, and his eyes fell to her mouth as though he couldn't possibly resist looking there. "In wishes."

He lifted a hand then, his fingers curving lightly—painfully lightly—around a clump of her pale hair. She held her breath as he tucked it behind her ear, his eyes transfixed by the small gesture.

"Yeah. I think I might."

And her lungs burned with the heat and strain of holding her breath, but she couldn't possibly exhale, she couldn't possibly breathe, she couldn't do anything except sit there and stare at him and feel every bit of magic in this incredible moment.

He dropped his head a little and anticipation throbbed through her veins. He pressed his forehead to Ally's, and she smiled softly, because the moment was filled with magic and wishes—how could she fail to believe in both?

He stayed like that, his forehead pressed to hers, and she kept smiling, until he slowly lifted his head up to stare into her eyes and something locked inside of her, something sharp and certain.

"I'm glad you came to Cape Hope."

The words from his note danced in her mind, thick with his husky voice now. Ally shifted her gaze to the inky night that surrounded them. The shooting star was gone, but the sky was no less beautiful for its absence.

She exhaled a shaky breath. "Me, too."

LUKE SMILED THE next day. A lot.

Stella had T-ball, and sitting in the bleachers with the other parents, he found his mind kept tracking over the dinner he'd shared with Amy and the way she'd moved, the way she'd cooked, the way she'd sipped her wine, the way her blue eyes had kept flicking to his. He'd wondered what it would be like to slow everything right down, stop moving, stop talking, to lean across the table and kiss her.

He thought back to the way they'd sat on the grass, a single blanket wrapped around them, their bodies so close together he could feel her softness and sweetness right beside him. He'd ached to wrap an arm around her shoulders and draw her even closer, to feel what it would be like to kiss her underneath the night sky he loved so much.

The stars above Cape Hope had seen his everything—his failures and successes, his joy and his despair, and now they were shimmering brightly above him, watching as he tentatively walked a path he thought he'd never tread again. He was falling—quickly, irrationally, unstoppably—into some kind of love, and even though he wanted to fight that, he felt the tug of this need, this fascination, and he knew the limit to his own powers. He couldn't put an end to this; he didn't really wish to.

Amy was only here for a short time. There was no easy, happy ending for him. The smart thing to do would be to walk away. Yet everything inside of him, and all the stars above him, were telling him to ignore sense, to throw caution deep into the wind, and abandon himself to this wild, tumbling fall—come what may.

"HOW'D YOU DO that?"

Ally paused midway through lifting the flour from the bag.

"Do what?"

Stella grinned and Ally was conscious of the way Luke was watching them from across the room. "Your hair? All braided like that."

Ally lifted a hand to the hair she'd plaited then pinned like a crown around her head, smiling at the six-year-old's innocent question. "Practice," she said simply.

"It's pretty."

"Thanks." Ally beamed, but her happiness was only partly because of the adorable sidekick she had in the kitchen. Mostly, it was because of the way Luke had greeted her at the door to his home that afternoon. She knew she hadn't been imagining the look that had passed from him to her.

He'd smiled at her in that way he had, and she'd smiled back, and it had been as though they were making a secret agreement, a pledge she didn't completely understand the terms of.

She'd come in, and he'd put on a blues playlist filled with guitar and deep, crooning vocals, and she'd chopped vegetables and chatted with Stella. But every few minutes she'd look toward Luke, whatever he was doing, and her heart would speed up a bit and anticipation trembled.

They were making a simple pasta bake and, even though Stella had wrinkled her nose when she'd seen all the vegetables Luke was grating—on Ally's instructions—for the sauce, by the time the thing was ready, she'd eaten it with gusto.

Over the rim of his wineglass, Luke's eyes met Ally's, and she smiled, slowly, carefully, and he simply stared at her, like there was a magnetic force locking his eyes to hers.

"This is so good," Stella confirmed as she scraped her bowl clean. "What else can we make?"

Warmth zipped inside Ally's chest. "I'll tell you what," she said thoughtfully. "Do you have any recipe books?"

"Dad does. But he's a terrible cook," Stella confided dubiously.

Luke and Ally laughed in unison. "Gee, thanks, butterfly," he said.

Stella pouted. "Well, you are."

"You didn't taste the chicken I roasted the other night. It was out of this world," he murmured, his eyes winging to Ally's once more, so all she could think of was the way it had felt to stand hip to hip with him in the kitchen, working on the meal together, how it had felt to sit beside him and stare at the stars, to be snuggled together under one small blanket. A tremble of something a lot like anticipation rolled down her spine.

"Beginner's luck," Stella volleyed back sharply, and Ally laughed once more, the phrase so unusual for a six-year-old that she could just hear Luke saying it. She liked the little girl's precociousness even when, at the same time, she could see how it might drive a parent just a teeny bit mad.

"Why don't you go get the cookbook?" Ally suggested, bringing the subject back to less-teasing ground. "And we'll choose something." She looked to Luke. "For next time."

They held each other's gaze as the meaning of those words landed around them. He quirked a brow, and her heart speeded up. What was she doing? This was too complicated. Too messy.

She wasn't staying long. Her old life beckoned, yet here she was, sitting opposite a man she couldn't stop thinking about, planning the next time they'd get to do this all over again.

"Okay!" Stella was up, bounding out of the room and into the hallway to a stack of shelves.

"Thanks for this," Luke said quietly, when they were alone.

"It's no problem. She's a good student."

"Better than me?" he joked.

"She's definitely less distracting." The words escaped before she could stop them, but Ally made no effort to hide what she'd meant, even as her cheeks grew hot.

He leaned forward a little, their eyes linking, and he reached over, his fingertips tracing a line on the back of her hand, so she sucked in a sharp breath of awareness. It was such a light touch, but he might as well have been lacing his fingers through hers and pulling her body to his—the impact was the same as if he had.

"Stella will be in bed in an hour. Do you want to…stick

around for a bit?"

Her heart began to rush faster—too fast. So fast she thought it might crack a rib or leap right out of her chest. "More stargazing?" The question was raspy, but her answer was already predetermined.

He tossed a glance over his shoulder, toward the dark, still evening. "It's a good night for it."

She couldn't resist a slightly disbelieving smile. "It's very cold."

He put his hand fully over hers now, and the smile died on Ally's lips. "I have more blankets." And then, with an expression that was completely serious, "I'll keep you warm."

So confident.

So sure.

So credible.

Ally sucked in a breath, nodding slowly, lost in that moment, lost completely. And she was lost. She'd come to Cape Hope to find her dad and, in doing so, had hoped to find a piece of herself that had always been missing, and instead, she was losing something in Luke. And she wasn't sure she even minded. "Okay."

"I got one!" Stella reappeared, and Luke's hand dropped from Ally's. She flexed her fingers to process the sudden sense of loss.

"Let me see." Somehow, her voice came out just a little thicker than normal.

"I like this one," Stella said, flipping the book open to a

recipe for gnocchi.

"Ah!" Ally forced herself to concentrate on Luke's daughter. "We can do this. Why don't you have a look at the ingredients and check them off against what you have in the fridge?" Ally prompted. "Make a list and let me know what you need more of."

Stella's face paled almost imperceptibly. "Can you help me?"

Ally was a little surprised by the request, but she pushed her chair back, smiling at Stella. "Sure."

They worked together, reading the ingredients and looking in the pantry and fridge for quantities. As she urged Stella to read the easier ingredients out, she noted the way Stella's face scrunched up with concentration, and the way she pressed her face right down, so her nose was practically touching the pages of the book.

By the time they were finished, the beginning of a suspicion had begun to form, one that she knew she should approach with delicacy—but it was something she had to address.

"You're so good with her," Luke remarked an hour or so later when Stella was fast asleep. Ally had filled the dishwasher while he'd read a book to Stella.

"She's easy to be with," Ally said honestly.

"Yeah, she's an angel with you," he admitted, a rough laugh escaping before he sobered, looking at Ally seriously. He closed the distance between them in the kitchen, and she held her breath, a thousand and one thoughts going through her mind, none that she could grasp. "And you're a really good cook."

Ally smiled distractedly. "Pasta bake isn't exactly a *croquembouche.*"

"Still." He shrugged as he got closer, and she bit down on her lower lip. He stopped a foot or so away from her, not touching, but close enough that if she reached out she could run her hands over his chest.

"Have you ever noticed her hesitation with reading?" Ally asked gently, her eyes roaming his face, hunger at war with concern.

His smile was dismissive. "She's stubborn. If she's not interested in something, she doesn't bother trying."

Ally thought about that. "Maybe," she conceded. "But have you ever wondered if maybe it's something more?"

That had him narrowing his gaze intently. "Like what?"

"I could be wrong, and I'm sorry if I am. It's just, watching her with the recipe book tonight, I wondered if maybe her vision isn't completely perfect." As soon as she said it, she worried she'd gone too far. People were sensitive about their kids—no one liked to be told their child wasn't perfect.

But Luke frowned, thinking that through, running over what he knew of his daughter. "I mean, her reading's behind. But I always thought it was just her small way of protesting the homework she's being given."

"Maybe it is," Ally rushed. "Only, she seemed to hold

her head really close to the pages as she was looking at the pictures, and when I asked her to read the list, she kept coming up with excuses not to. I almost felt she was guessing her way through the ingredient list. It's just a hunch."

His expression showed he was listening, that he was taking her seriously. She was glad. "I'll look into it."

And she was pretty sure he meant it. "I'm sorry to worry you."

"Don't be. I appreciate you speaking up."

"I could be wrong."

"Or, you could be right." And now, he took a step closer, so their hips were touching. He looked down at her and she held her breath, looking up at him. He laced his fingers through hers, their hands at their sides. "Amy," he said quietly, stroking the back of her hand.

Crap.

She closed her eyes against the name she'd given him a week ago, a name it hadn't occurred to her to mind using. But she hated it now. She hated that she'd lied to him; she hated that she felt trapped by that lie. She opened her mouth, needing to tell him the truth, wanting him to understand the lie had started out harmless, a fib of self-protection, and had become a noose around her neck.

But he spoke before she could, his voice gruff and throaty. "I haven't been with anyone in a long time. Since Jen." He frowned in a way that made him—somehow—even more beautiful, more fascinating, more intense. Ally's chest hurt with how many emotions were bursting through her. His voice cracked a little. "I didn't think I'd ever be with anyone again."

Ally's ribs tightened. She had to tell him the truth before this went any further. "Luke…"

Except she didn't finish the sentence. His name hung between them, an entreaty to listen, but only silence finished.

He carried on after a few beats, his words racked with an intensity that pulled at every single cell in her body. "But with you, I can't… I feel…" He shook his head, the right words failing him. "I really like being with you."

Breath burned in her lungs. *Crap.* She really liked being with him, too, and she hadn't banked on any of this when she'd come to Cape Hope. She didn't want this complication.

"And I find myself looking at you…"

"Yes?" Her own voice was a barely there husk.

"I find myself looking at you." He lifted a hand to her cheek, stroking it with his fingertips before cupping it with his palm. "And wanting to kiss you."

Ridiculously, she felt the sting of tears.

"All the time." He grimaced wryly, moving his body closer, so she felt the strength and hardness of his frame. "I mean, you're really funny and smart and a fantastic cook." His words were lighthearted, but he didn't smile. "But really, I'm just standing here thinking about what you'd say if I kissed you."

She sucked in an uneven breath, her lips tingling, wishing, wanting, needing him to do exactly that.

"And I know I shouldn't. Because you're not here for keeps, and I don't want Stella getting attached to someone who's just temporary in our lives, you know?"

Desperation to fix this, to tell him the truth or somehow take it back, to tell him the real reason she was in North Carolina, flooded her, but so did so many other feelings, and she didn't know which to listen to. Because there was fear, too. Fear that if he knew she'd lied, he'd feel differently. And an even deeper worry that, if he knew even her own dad hadn't loved her enough to stay around, he might see that maybe she wasn't that great after all.

She swallowed past the vulnerability she hated, nodding instead, her eyes awash with confusion. "That makes sense."

"But it doesn't, Amy. It doesn't make sense, because kissing you is all that I can think about, and I want, more than anything, just to ignore what I know I *should* do, and give in to *this*."

Uncertainty was a firework bursting through her. She owed him so much more than this. She was *lying* to him! And it hadn't mattered when he was just a handsome man outside a diner, a helpful stranger at the fair, or the handyman who'd been sent to her holiday rental to take care of a maintenance problem. But now that he was marching inside of her and stealing a piece of her heart, it mattered a whole lot.

"Luke." She bit down on her lip, and he studied the gesture. She felt his question, his need, his wants, and they so perfectly matched her own that, in spite of everything she knew, of how wrong she knew this to be, she couldn't fight it. Not even for a second.

She pushed up on her tiptoes, the tiny gesture enough of an invitation that he understood, and he answered in the only way he could.

As though the wall of a dam had burst, he claimed her mouth with his own, holding her body tight to his, and all the doubts slipped through the cracks of her being in the face of such certainty and perfection. Yes, she knew this wasn't easy, and she knew it wasn't ideal, but the second he kissed her, she also knew that this was bigger than him or her, bigger than them. Some kind of force was at work, pushing them together, and she wasn't going to fight it.

They kissed, and the world tilted sideways. They kissed, and the stars outside sparkled, the night air chilled, the house stood watch as it had done for over a century.

They kissed as though it were simple, and hoped maybe it would be.

Chapter Nine

HE'D FELT REALLY guilty about a lot of stuff these past six years. He'd felt guilty about his terrible skills in the hair department. All the other girls started first grade with neat buns or braids, and Stella had stood there, her ponytail full of bumps and stray hairs, no ribbon, no headband. He'd felt guilty about how he couldn't cook any of the things she liked and how he lost his temper. He felt guilty about the fact she only had one parent. He felt guilty a lot of the time.

But nothing compared to the guilt he felt now, sitting opposite Stella in the diner, a new pair of bright-pink glasses perched on the bridge of her nose.

How the hell had he missed this?

Amy had spent approximately three seconds with his daughter and saw what he should have noticed years ago.

"They kinda hurt my ears."

If he could carry this burden for her, he would. More guilt. "The optician said they might at first."

"I know. I can't see properly, I can hear just fine."

He bit back a smile, but his heart squeezed for her with an aching vulnerability. "It's a minor vision impairment that might even correct itself with age."

She nodded, a tentative smile on her face. "Do you think I look stupid?"

Her voice was a little trembly, so unlike her usual self, and his heart broke for her. He reached across the table, putting his hand over hers. "I think you're the most beautiful girl in the world."

She sucked in a breath, nodding a little uncertainly, turning to catch her reflection in the mirrored walls that lined their booth before jerking her head around to look behind her. "Look, it's Amy!"

He followed her gaze, his body instantly tightening in response. Amy. A smile spread slowly over his face as anticipation warmed him right through. She was bundled up against the cold—skinny jeans, a sweater, beanie, scarf and coat, boots that were slim and fitted to her ankle. He watched as she approached the counter, takeout coffee cup in hand. His pulse was faster than a cheetah.

"Do you think she'll like my glasses?"

"Why don't you go and ask her?" he suggested, groaning inwardly at the act of cowardice in sending his six-year-old daughter as his ambassador.

Still. It had been two nights since they'd kissed. He hadn't called her—he'd wanted to give her space. But she hadn't called him, either.

He'd checked his phone a hundred times, but there was nothing, and he hadn't known what to do. That was, in and of itself, completely uncharacteristic, and more evidence—like he needed any—that something weird was happening between them, and with him. It wasn't like the other women who'd asked him out.

She was different.

He was on tenterhooks as Stella skipped across the diner, tapping Amy on the hip and waiting with her hands behind her back.

Amy paused what she was doing and turned to Stella, her expression a mixture of surprise and pleasure at seeing the little girl, then she scanned the restaurant, automatically looking for him.

Their gazes locked and she smiled; his stomach shifted. He unfurled from the seat, striding across the restaurant to the two of them, trying not to indulge stupid thoughts like how good they looked together, trying to remind himself Amy wasn't in town for long, that whatever this was, she was like a Christmas guardian angel or something. Someone who'd come to Cape Hope and would leave again just as quickly, but in the meantime, she was a part of their lives, and he was glad for that.

"I was just complimenting Stella on her glasses," she said with a smile.

"She picked them out herself."

"I thought so."

"I like pink," Stella said, but seriously, so Ally responded in kind, nodding sagely.

"And pink likes you."

"Colors can't like people."

"I beg to differ."

"We were just about to order dinner. A sort of celebratory meal," Luke expanded. "Would you"—he hesitated—"like to join us?"

Amy's eyes met his and warmth moved gently between them. "I'd like that very much."

They walked as a trio back to the booth and, when they were almost there, Luke's hand brushed against Amy's. She lifted her head to his, smiling a little.

He smiled back, anticipation a wave in his chest, and excitement, too—excitement for the first time in a really long time.

Amy moved to sit beside Stella, and he was glad for that, glad she was being careful to guard against it looking like they were a couple, or giving Stella any kind of hope along those lines. Whatever was happening between them was new and exciting, but he had no idea where it would go—where it *could* even go, given she was from several states away.

Stella talked a thousand miles a minute. She wasn't even quiet when she reviewed the menu. "Smoky mac and cheese, please."

Luke lifted his brow. "You sure? No cheeseburger?"

Stella smiled, moving her head from side to side. More guilt—had she really been ordering a cheeseburger every time because she couldn't make out the rest of the menu?

"And for you, madam?" He turned to Amy, his gut lurching at the sight of her squished in beside Stella. She was an incredibly attractive woman, but it was so much more than that. He loved her smile and her laugh, the little divot between her brows when she was lost in thought. It was the deft movements of her hands as she cooked; it was the way she listened to him like her whole soul's survival depended on what he was saying, the way she spun stories as she spoke, stories he needed to know.

"Hmm, I don't know if I can go past the crab with blue cheese sauce."

Luke grinned. "Done. To drink?"

"Just a soda, thanks."

He stood up, looking down at the two of them, something shifting in his chest. "Don't get up to any trouble, you two."

"Yessir," Stella said with an expression that was pure trouble, and as he walked toward the counter to order he heard giggling—Stella's and Amy's—and he had to focus hard not to keep turning around to look at them. But there was something magnetic about the sight of them together, something that clicked like a puzzle piece falling into place, and it wasn't about Amy, it was about him, and what his future would look like if he ever decided to tread this path again.

This was a huge part of it.

Needing to know that whoever he fell in love with fell

just as much in love with Stella as they did with him. He wasn't a lone ranger, acting on his own gut instincts. Whoever he decided to care for and get involved with would be joining a family.

That was a big deal.

But he liked the look of that—of Amy and Stella sitting together, talking, a huge smile on Stella's newly bespectacled face—so he felt an overwhelming rush of pleasure at what it was like to have someone else in their lives. For a moment, he let himself imagine that it was permanent. He let himself imagine way down the road, meeting often at the diner, first, then coming here together, from his place.

He froze, frowning, because the thought was way out of left field and shouldn't have even been on his radar. It wasn't an option. She was a tourist. She was just visiting. This wasn't a "forever" kind of thing.

But what if it could be?

He rubbed his palm over his chin, the thought one he knew he should push away but found he couldn't. She had no plans to stay. But plans changed. What did she have waiting for her back home?

He ordered a burger and fries for himself, some onion rings for the table, and found his gaze shifting to the mural to his right, remembering how excited Jen had been when she'd written to tell him about it. She'd loved painting Cape Hope on a wall. And she'd done a damned fine job. Somehow she'd captured the essence of dozens of townspeople, a living time capsule of what life had been like in Cape Hope then. He walked toward it on autopilot, concentrating on the faces he knew as well as anything, landing finally on the sketch of him and Jen, Stella just a promise in her belly at that point in time.

He'd spent six years missing her, and he'd always thought he'd stay single forever, partly because no woman could ever replace Jen in his heart, and partly because he felt like he owed it to her. To miss her and mourn her forever. It seemed like the least he could do.

For six years he'd found it easy to be single, and now, almost every waking thought revolved around the beautiful stranger who'd blown into Cape Hope and exploded his every idea of who he was and what he wanted.

"What would you think?" he murmured quietly, studying Jen's self-drawn portrait, even though he could picture it with his eyes shut. "Would you like her?"

But he knew the answer to that. Jen would have loved her, and all the more for seeing how good the woman was with their daughter. He turned his back on the mural, focusing on the table once more—only to see Jen's brother, Jacob, standing with Stella and Amy, his back to the restaurant dining room, but instantly recognizable for the sheriff's uniform he wore.

Luke strolled over, his hands in his pockets until he got close enough to clap Jacob on the back. "Hey, buddy. You on the night shift?"

Jacob turned to Luke, something a little strange in his expression. "Yeah. Just catching up with Stella here."

"And meeting Amy," Stella said, batting her lashes.

Luke nodded, wondering at the metallic taste that fired in his mouth before comprehension dawned. He'd just been thinking about how good a future would look with this woman, and here she was meeting his late wife's brother.

It was something he hadn't really contemplated—it wasn't just about him and Stella; there were others. Family members who'd loved and lost Jen, whose lives had been as shaped by that loss as his own had been.

"So you're just passing through town?" Jacob prompted, his demeanor relaxed. Only Luke, who knew Jacob so well, could perceive a hint of tension in his shoulders.

"Yeah," Amy responded simply, her smile barely a flicker on her lips.

"How'd you meet these two?"

Before she could answer, Stella jumped in. "Amy's teaching us to cook."

"Seriously?" At this, Jacob grinned, turning to face Luke, a look of pure disbelief on his features. "This guy?" He hitched his thumb at Luke.

Luke rolled his eyes. "I'm not a complete loss in the kitchen."

"Oh, Daddy." Stella giggled indulgently and even Amy had to hide a smile behind the back of her hand.

"You need a little help," Amy said diplomatically.

"So you're some kind of traveling cooking school?" Jacob questioned.

"What's with the third degree, Sheriff?" The question was lighthearted enough, but Luke felt impatient.

"Just making small talk."

He was pretty sure it was more than that, but didn't push it. "Want to join us? I've just ordered."

Jacob's eyes drifted to Amy's, his expression thoughtful. "Nah. I'm just grabbing a quick coffee. I'll see you next week?"

"Count on it."

"Nice to meet you, Amy," he said, leaning forward and shaking her hand without cracking a smile. Was it any wonder she looked a little stricken? Jacob was acting as though she was a potential fugitive or something. He'd have to talk to his brother-in-law. Jacob turned his attention to Stella and his demeanor visibly altered, his smile genuine, his eyes warm. "Fist bump, butterfly."

Jacob sauntered toward the counter, leaving them alone. Amy's eyes met Luke's, and there was appraisal there, a thoughtfulness that he wanted to investigate—and would do later.

He owed her an explanation, or something. Jacob wasn't usually so rude. He could be gruff as all get-out, and he was definitely no-nonsense, but he was also kind and fair, and yet he'd treated Amy with suspicion, and she'd obviously noticed.

"What are you doing for Christmas?" Stella asked when their food had arrived and she was partway through her mac and cheese.

"Me?" Amy paused, grabbing her napkin and wiping her hands. She ate crab like someone who lived for food, and a knot in Luke's gut formed because he wasn't sure he'd ever seen anything sweeter.

"Yeah, you." Stella nodded, not smiling.

Amy's expression was tight suddenly, her features showing strain. "I hadn't really thought about it," she said. A sense of disquiet moved through him. She'd mentioned she was going home for Christmas, and it hadn't bothered him then, but now it filled him with the beginning of disquiet, a sense of apprehension he didn't welcome.

"Why not?"

"I'm not sure."

"Well, do you have a tree and go to church and then your mom and dad's? I'll bet you cook something yummy."

"I do, usually," she agreed, her tone flattened of the emotions that he instinctively knew she was feeling. "But I'm not sure about this year."

"Why not?"

Sympathy perforated his gut at the sight of Amy's throat moving as she swallowed past her feelings. "My mom died a few months ago," she said gently.

Stella's expression was serious beyond her years. "My mom died, too."

Amy stroked the little girl's hair, and the simple gesture of comfort warmed Luke from the inside out. "Yeah, I know."

"I never knew her."

Amy's eyes shifted to Luke's for a moment. "I bet your dad tells you lots about her, though."

Stella's grin was full of enthusiasm. "Yep. And how much we're alike."

Luke's heart was too big for his body suddenly.

Stella reached for the salt shaker, running her fingertip over the little holes in the top distractedly. "What did you and your mom do for Christmas?"

"Normally, she'd come over to my place the night before and sleep over." Amy's eyes assumed a faraway look.

"Even though you're a grown-up?"

Amy smiled and nodded.

"You don't have a husband?"

"No husband."

"A boyfriend?"

"Nope."

Something like possessiveness and pride flared in his chest. Danger lights flared.

"Oh. Why not?"

Amy laughed, picking up a crab claw and cracking it like a pro. "I guess I just never met anyone I liked enough."

It was ridiculous to feel pleasure at that, given they'd only kissed once, and yet he did.

He knew what he wanted and where his thoughts were taking him; there was a future on the periphery of his mind, and Amy was in it, front and center. "What would you and your mom do? Christmas Eve?" he asked, leaning forward without meaning to.

Amy's eyes flicked to his. "I'd make eggnog—I make a mean eggnog." This was murmured to Stella with a quick smile. "And we'd watch the same movie every year."

"What movie?"

"*An Affair to Remember.*" She sighed.

"I don't know it," Stella said, frowning.

"I'm not surprised. It's super old. But so good. I cry every time."

"A sad movie?"

"Poignant," she corrected thoughtfully.

"What's that?"

"Kind of happy-sad."

"Ah."

"So you'll watch it by yourself this year?" Stella pushed, a look on her face that showed how little she thought of this plan.

"I don't know." Amy shook her head, her tender pain easy to see.

"I don't think you should do that," Stella continued, turning to Luke and fixing him with a determined stare. "Daddy, I think Amy should stay with us for Christmas."

Amy's eyes showed alarm now. "That's so sweet, Stella,"

she said gently. "But Christmas is a time for family, and you guys should be together."

"We will be together."

"Without outsiders."

"You're our friend," Stella insisted. "Right, Dad?"

"Right," Luke agreed, without missing a beat. And with a growing sense of determination that threw every bit of caution he knew he should be exercising to the wind, he offered, "I'm sure you've probably got friends back home, but if you change your mind about staying in town, we'd love to have you." Amy's fingers toyed with the crab claw, and Luke put a hand over hers. Just for a moment, so fast that it escaped Stella's notice. "You'd be welcome."

Emotions charged her expression, and her smile was soft. "Thanks. But I'll be back in Madison for Christmas." The words were bleak and lacking any enthusiasm. She dropped her eyes to the crab, and his stomach clenched, uncertainty homing in on excitement's terrain.

Christmas was only two weeks away.

He didn't want her to be gone by then.

He was all kinds of stupid to be getting involved in this—he was in way, way over his head. He told himself this was just a fling, a flirtation, getting back on the dating-horse. All the while, visions of future plums danced in his head.

"We haven't even got our tree up yet," Stella pointed out thoughtfully.

Inwardly, Luke winced. Yeah, he'd dropped the ball

there, too.

"That's okay, it's only mid-December still." Amy cracked the crab claw, and a heap of gunk spat out and dashed across Luke's cheek. Stella burst out laughing, and Amy smothered a gasp and then giggled.

His heart splintered at the picture of them so happy together, even if it was most definitely at his expense. He kept his eyes on Amy's as he reached for a napkin and wiped his face clean, a smile playing around his lips.

"I'm sorry." She giggled again, with Stella still laughing beside her.

"You two are quite the team, you know that?"

Amy's eyes widened and flew to Stella's. Stella leaned closer to her in a spontaneous hug. "Yup. We are."

Danger bells pealed.

Two weeks. Not even. Playing happy family was stupid, stupid, stupid. He needed to pull this back. He knew what he should do. And yet…hell.

He loved this.

Everything felt good and warm and it'd been a long time since he could have said that about anything.

"We'll go out to Heyworth's on the weekend, pick our tree," he promised Stella. And then he heard himself ask, his voice all low and gruff, "Why don't you come with us, crabby fingers?"

Amy swallowed, and her huge blue eyes locked to his. For a second he thought she was going to say no. He could feel the battle being waged inside of her, a battle just like his own, maybe even for similar reasons. She was blowing out of town just as quickly as she'd blown into it. Christmas tree shopping? Like a family? It was a stupid idea.

"A real tree?"

He arched a brow. "Yeah."

She turned to look out the window. It was dark out, the street glowing from the beautiful lights that were strung over the street every winter. He could feel that same fight being fought within her, and he sat completely still, his breath held as though that could sway the result.

"Please." Stella tugged on Amy's arm. "It'll be fun. We'll choose a really big tree, and then you can make eggnog while we decorate it."

He felt the tug of his own heart and knew—somehow—that Amy's was reverberating in the same way. Because when she turned to face him, it was like she was fighting tears. "That sounds awfully nice."

"So Saturday?" he suggested before she could change her mind.

There was a pause, one that ramped up his tension, his worry that she might say 'no'. "Okay, Saturday."

He expelled a soft breath. "Great." His smile was impulsive. "I'm looking forward to it." Understatement of the century.

After Stella finished her dinner, she asked to go sit with the Millers a few booths back. "Yeah, if it's okay with Kitty."

"I'll ask," Stella promised, sliding out from the booth and skipping off. They watched her jog over, and a second later, her little voice drifted back their way. "She said it's okay!"

Luke laughed, leaning back in his chair, meeting Amy's eyes over his beer.

"She's a really sweet little girl," Amy said with obvious sincerity in her voice.

"She can be."

"I don't believe she ever has a bad attitude."

"Oh, she does." He laughed, tilting his head back, unaware of the way Amy's eyes lingered on his lips and then his throat, nor the way her cheeks flushed pink. He dropped his head forward, running his hand through his hair. "But the optometrist said she'll probably be a different kid now."

"Really?"

"Yeah. Apparently, with how bad her eyes were, she'd have been straining all day just to make sense of her school work." His expression was rueful. "Want to have a guess how crappy I feel?"

"Oh, you shouldn't." Amy propped her elbows on the tabletop, her eyes scanning his face earnestly.

"Really? It took you no time at all to realize what was right under my nose. I'm her dad; I should have known."

"There's a lot worse things a dad can do to his daughter, believe me," she murmured, the words heavy with emotions.

Luke was silent, thinking of this beautiful woman's father and the way he'd run out on her, and the scars that kind of desertion would leave. "I know." Two small, insufficient words, when he wanted to say he was sorry she'd gone through that, sorry she'd had to know the pain and disappointment of having her dad abandon her. "I just feel like I should have seen something."

"Were there are any other signs?"

"Now that I know she needed glasses? Loads. I just didn't connect the dots. That's not like me. I'm usually pretty in tune."

She was quiet for a moment, her eyes frustratingly closed to him, her attention drawn by the drink in front of her. She stared at it for several beats, her features taut, her face a mask of concentration. What was she thinking about? He wanted to know; he wanted to ask. But there was something completely closed off, something that warned him not to intrude.

A second later, she relaxed a little, responding to his statement as though no time had passed. "It takes an outside perspective sometimes," Amy promised, lifting her eyes to his. "I've heard my mom go through this same thing with lots of kids. It's way more common than you'd think."

"Really?" He cheered a little.

"Yep." She turned in the direction of the family Stella had joined. "You seem like a really great dad."

Her words were a balm he hadn't known he needed. It was incredibly easy to doubt himself most days. "I think I'm flying blind half the time."

"I'm sure all single parents feel like that."

He scrunched his nose for a second, kicking his legs straight out beneath him, until the toes of his boots brushed against her ankles and she sat up a little taller, her expression so full of surprise and raw need that his gut rolled. Their eyes met and he felt like he was sinking—and he was glad.

He didn't move his feet, nor did she hers.

"I know my mom always thought she was doing it wrong," Amy continued, but her voice was different—higher in pitch. Longing passed between them.

He struggled to rally his thoughts back to this conversation. "I'm lucky. Cape Hope is a good place to do this on my own. The town is supportive—everyone knows everything. I feel like I have a thousand pseudo-parents ready to give me advice or help."

"That sounds like a double-edged sword." She sat back against the vinyl booth seats and shifted her feet a little, crossing her legs at the knees so the toe of one of her shoes brushed against his calf. He had no idea if it was by accident, but the effect was the same. Desire surged in his body. "I guess there are some times you don't want anyone's help."

His smile was wry. "Not as often as you'd think."

But there was something in her expression, something serious and intense. "Isn't there ever something you want to keep to yourself?"

His lips pulled downward. "Like what?"

She drew in a breath, slowly, her nostrils flaring in her

sweet face. "I guess…private stuff. I mean, there must be some things you don't want people to know."

"Nah, I'm an open book." He lifted his beer and took a drink. "That's the only way to be in a small town like this."

She nodded, but he felt her doubts.

"Cities are different," he pointed out. "You make your own community, find your tribe, all that stuff."

"Yeah." She still didn't seem convinced.

"Do you think you could ever live in a small town?" Damn it. Her expression closed up altogether, something like panic easy to discern in her expressive eyes. He was being too full on, too intense. Not for the first time, he wanted to kick himself for his lack of experience with dating.

It's not a date.

Sure it's not.

"I doubt it." The words held a warning—to him, or to her?

He needed to change the conversation before their night tanked. He didn't want her to look cold and distant. He needed her to smile again. He made an effort to affect a look of relaxation, to lull her into a similar state. "I'm glad you spoke up with what you'd seen. I owe you."

"Yeah?" She was still quiet.

"Yeah." Damn it. He needed to fix this. He wanted another shot. "What are you doing tomorrow morning?"

She swallowed, her throat moving visibly. "I…nothing. Why?"

He leaned forward and laced his fingers through hers. "Want to do something?"

They were being pulled into a gravity well, but they were being pulled together. "Like what?"

"How about a walk on the beach?"

She tilted her head to the side, her lips parted a little, her eyes roaming his face like she was looking for a way to say no. Like she was wishing it was already morning. He needed this. More time with her. More time to understand her.

"I'll bring breakfast rolls and coffee," he added, sweetening the deal.

He waited with no degree of patience whatsoever. Beneath the table, he slid his hand over his knee, his fingers drumming against his kneecap, his expression blanked of what he was feeling.

"I'd like that."

Relief was immediate. But there was doubt, too. "You're sure?"

She laughed unsteadily, then latched their eyes. "No." She propped her cheek in her palm, staring at him for several beats of time. "I'm not sure this isn't completely crazy; in fact, I have absolutely no idea what I'm doing, but I don't seem to be able to say no to you, Luke."

His heart did a few extra beats. He grinned, and now, his feet rubbed her ankles intentionally. "I'm kind of glad to hear it."

"SO, YOU'RE DATING or something?"

Maybe calling Jacob had been a bad idea. Luke expelled a soft sigh, padding barefoot across the living room and picking up his guitar, phone nestled between his ear and shoulder. He strummed a chord, thinking of Amy, and smiled spontaneously. "I wouldn't say that."

"You looked like you were into her."

Luke thought about denying it, but he didn't believe in lying, and not to people he loved. "And? Is there something wrong with that? With her?"

Silence crackled down the phone line, and Luke stilled, his fingers resting on the guitar's fret. "I don't know," Jacob admitted finally.

Sympathy shifted inside Luke, but there was impatience, too, because he'd been single and celibate for six years. He wasn't exactly rushing into this. So what if it could only ever be a fling? Didn't he deserve even that? "She's not here long," Luke said in an effort to placate his brother-in-law.

"So?"

"So..." He strummed the guitar once more, not smiling now. "It's not serious."

Another crackly silence. "That's even weirder."

"Weirder?" Luke pulled a face. "What's weird about this?"

"She's on vacation in Cape Hope. She's a tourist. What

business does she have getting all involved in your life?"

"I involved her." The second he said the words, he knew he was prepared to go toe-to-toe with his best friend and brother-in-law. He knew Amy was worth it.

"Who even is she? What do you know about her?"

I know she has a smile that could light up the sky. I know she's beautiful and funny and cooks great. I know she's orphaned and alone. I know I love spending time with her. I know she's just like me in all the ways that matter, that she makes whatever's broken inside of me feel shiny and new again.

Luke sighed heavily. "It's been six years, man."

Silence.

"I loved Jen. If I could have died to save her, you know I would have. A thousand times, I would have." His voice was deep with the strength of his emotions. "But I've been living in some kind of stasis since she died. I'm sick of being alone. For the first time in six years, I have someone to talk to. Someone to share things with. Someone I wake up and want to call first thing in the morning, just to hear the sound of her voice. I can't get her out of my head, Jacob. And I'm sorry if that sucks for you. Believe me, I feel like I'm cheating on Jen half the time, too. But I can't not do this. I don't *want* to not do this." Luke gripped the phone even tighter, his outburst unexpected, tension in the taut line of his shoulders. But there was freedom in his admission, freedom in admitting to himself and his best friend the truth of what Amy had come to mean to him.

"It was just strange. Seeing you with someone else, you

know?"

Luke's focus was drawn to the photo of Jen and him on their wedding day. "Yeah, buddy. I know."

"It was strange seeing you *happy* with someone else," Jacob corrected. "That makes me a kind of selfish ass, I know."

Luke laughed gruffly, rubbing his jaw. "Yeah, but you're the best selfish ass I know."

Chapter Ten

NOT LONG AFTER Jack Monroe had walked out of the house, never to return, Ally's mother had destroyed every single picture of him. Ally hadn't noticed at first—kids didn't generally care for those sorts of details. One day, pictures started disappearing off walls. The wedding photo Ally saw so often she no longer paid attention to it. The picture of Jack and a pink newborn Ally. Jack smiling, looking out toward the camera, the sun catching the longer hairs at the back of his neck.

All the pictures had disappeared, and later, when Ally had been older, maybe ten or eleven, she'd gone looking for a photo album on a whim, wondering about Jack, yes, but also about her own childhood—how many of her memories were real and how many make-believe, influenced by televisions shows, books, and friends' narratives.

She'd gone looking for the albums her mom kept in a plastic box at the bottom of the closet, only they weren't there. No albums. No photos. Just an empty square of carpet where a box used to sit.

She'd asked her mom about it later that day and, without

missing a beat, Sasha had responded. *They're gone. Good riddance to bad garbage.*

It hadn't occurred to Ally to mind. She'd felt momentarily put out, but had been distracted easily enough, content to leave the question of her memory's accuracy for another day.

It was only a couple of years after that, when things had become better financially and they'd moved from the apartment to a house—a bigger house with a garden and a porch and a nice next-door neighbor—that Ally had come across the last remaining photographic evidence that she did indeed have a father—and that he looked just as she'd remembered.

The picture had been wedged under a sofa cushion, a photograph of a long-forgotten time. Like gold dust. She'd lifted it up, transfixed, staring at the smiling face of the man she'd loved, and it had been like a horse rearing and kicking her right in the ribs. She'd staggered back a step until her hip connected with her desk, unable to take her eyes from the photo.

And she'd known it was gold dust but also contraband, that her mother wouldn't like seeing the photo. So she'd stuffed it in her backpack and kept it there, her secret treasure.

She carried it inside her leather journal now, slipped between the dust jacket and front cover. With a funny feeling, she pulled it out and propped it against the fruit bowl so she could look directly at it as she drank her coffee.

He'd changed—he'd aged—but there was more to it than that. The man in the photo looked…broken. She'd never thought that as a child, but now Ally could see something in her father's face that made sympathy move through her soul. She pitied this man, and whoever he'd been, whatever had made him run. But he wasn't like that anymore. At least, he didn't seem to be. In the restaurant, he'd looked like someone full of life and confidence.

He'd looked…happy.

Emotions were threatening to suffocate her. She stood up abruptly, pacing from one side of the kitchen to the other.

She'd come all this way to confront her father, so why did she keep chickening out? Why couldn't she march up to that kitchen window and give him a piece of her mind? Tears filled her eyes, and she groaned, dashing them away impatiently looking back to the photo as though she couldn't help herself.

She'd known him for less than one quarter of her life, and yet he continued to have this hold over her. Every day she lived and breathed, his shadow cut through her, and the fact that her own father had chosen not to be a part of her life was a reality she knew she had to live with.

Yet the day after a lonely, quiet Thanksgiving—with none of the usual trimmings—she'd packed up her car and driven here, and all she could think about was the kid she'd been, who'd needed, more than anything, for her daddy to stay and love her. He'd walked away from her like she meant nothing, but nothing could change the fact Jack Monroe remained an anchor point of sorts for Ally.

She needed to confront him—not to punish him or make him feel a guilt he clearly didn't have, but because in showing him she was still here, a real person, an adult now, she might finally be able to cut that anchor loose, to sever him from her life, to diminish his importance, and move forward—move on—without him in her mind in the same kind of way. Without this feeling of worthlessness and shame that had dogged her every step.

And so she swore that, the very next time she went into Beauty Falls, it would be the last time—because she'd do what she'd come to North Carolina to achieve, and that would be the end of this.

She could go home—mystery solved.

❦

THE THOUGHT GAVE her little pleasure, and even less so as she spent the morning with Luke Miller.

They walked along the beach, talking about Stella and the town, his local knowledge impressive and fascinating. He pointed out lots of little features and details as they went, described ships that had run aground off the coastline. He spoke with pride and affection, and all she could think about was how perfect he was. How any other time, in any other place, she might have let herself fall in love with him and imagine the kind of future she knew to be utterly impossible.

"I'm boring you, right?" he asked, and she jerked her face to his, her heart skipping as she saw him and felt an impossible pull to him. The sun was right behind him, casting him in gold. "What can I say? I'm very proud of this place."

She didn't smile. She lifted a hand to his chest, urgency propelling her forward. "Luke..."

His own expression mirrored hers, serious and intent; he didn't speak. But then he lifted a hand, catching a clump of her hair as it flew in the breeze, and her stomach rolled and her arms pricked with goosebumps that had nothing to do with the frigid winter's morning.

She swept her eyes shut for a second, reality washing over her. He didn't even know her name. What was she doing? "I didn't come here to get involved with anyone."

His smile was a devastatingly handsome twist of his lips. "Is that what we're doing?"

Ally didn't say that she was afraid of what they were doing, because if she had to imagine what falling in love would be like, it would go a lot like this. "I'm serious."

He nodded. "I know." He dropped his hand but stayed close, so close she could sway forward and touch him. "Don't you think I've been thinking about this, too? I haven't been with anyone since Jen died. I've focused all of myself on being a good dad to Stella, and I always thought, in the back of my mind, that if I started dating, I'd be so sensible about it, making sure it was for keeps before I let anyone get to know me or my daughter. And then I met you and everything's happened so fast and all out of order and I can't stop it, Amy. I don't *want* to stop it." He caught her face in his hands then, the wind whipping around them, making their clothes shift and strain at their bodies. "I don't want to stop this even though I know you're leaving, and I'm going to hate that. But you know what I'll hate even more?"

"What?" She groaned, her eyes moving over his face hungrily, her body conscious only of his warmth in contrast to the cold day.

"Not doing this, not making the most of having you here." He shook his head slowly, and she felt him sinking into the reality of this futile situation—she recognized it because it was just how she felt. "I told myself I should walk away from whatever this is, Amy, but God help me, I can't."

Amy. It should have been like a wake-up call, an urgent imperative to stir her to sense and rational thought, but nothing could penetrate the urgent fog of her wanting, longing.

He dropped his forehead to hers, and she sucked in an uneven breath. "I can't."

"Nor can I," she whispered.

With a soft breath, she tilted her face, and he captured her mouth in his, kissing her longingly, achingly, imperfectly, because his words were inside of her, and she wanted to cry for how right this was in the midst of knowing it to be wrong.

He kissed her, and happiness and longing surged in her breast.

"Come back to the cottage with me," she offered simply, the invitation about so much more than geography. He nodded, and she smiled, the future something they'd deal with later, next week, or the week after. It would be there waiting for them, but for now there was just this, and it was more than enough.

❦

SHE LAY WITH her head against his chest, listening to the beating of his heart, staring at the walls of Cardinal Cottage, feeling no awkwardness, no regret. She lay with her head on his chest, their limbs entwined, and all she could think about was the sublime perfection of this day.

They'd driven to the cottage in silence, but a silence heavy with anticipation and knowing—they'd danced around this for days and desire had been impossible to fight, need overtaking them. The door to the house had only just clicked shut before he'd lifted her in his arms, holding her tight to his body, kissing her as though his life had depended on it, and she'd fallen through the cracks of sanity into a world that was pure pleasure and temptation. He'd held her to his chest and carried her up the stairs, shouldering open the door to the bedroom, and they'd taken one another's clothes off reverently, slowly, both staving off a furious desire to see and touch and feel with a pleasure in prolonging the slow, torturous intimacy.

Ally had dated a few guys, each of them wildly unsuitable. Bad guys, bastards who'd told her she'd never amount to much, guys who were all wrong for her, guys who made it easy to push them away.

She'd never felt anything like this.

She'd never slept with someone who connected with her in every way. It was blissful, intoxicating, and addictive.

They'd made love for hours, and now she lay beside him, so comfortable she could drift off to sleep. His hand stroked her naked back, and she smiled, contentment wrapping around her like a lovely illustration of a cloud.

"I really am glad you came to Cape Hope," he observed, his voice rumbling in her ear.

Ally pushed up onto her elbow, studying his face when she knew it as well as she did her own. *Tell him why you're really here.* Her stomach flip-flopped. "Me, too."

He lifted a hand and ran it over her shoulder lightly, his eyes following the trail his fingers made against her smooth flesh. "I never thought I'd feel like this again." The words were said with such raw honesty, his voice deep in tone.

Ally's smile was lopsided, and all too brief. "I never thought I'd feel like this at all."

His eyes narrowed speculatively. "No?" She shook her head, and he closed the distance between them, kissing her so she lost the ability to think momentarily. "I like being able to do that." He smiled against her mouth and she felt herself smile back. "I've been thinking about kissing you since I saw you outside the diner."

"No way." She laughed.

"Yeah." He drew his hand lower, over her hip, resting it there a moment. "I was actually jealous of Matt, that night at the fair."

It took her a second to remember the other resident who'd shown her around. "Seriously?"

He grinned, and her heart buckled. His smile was so nice. So warm. So mesmerizing. "Yep."

"Well, if it makes you feel any better, I haven't really been able to stop thinking about you since that night."

It was a mistake. Oh, it was how she felt. It was the God's honest truth. But it was also a lie, because it offered something she couldn't give him; it spoke of the lure of a permanence that was beyond them.

She shifted her head a little, just enough to convey her consternation. For goodness' sake, he didn't even know her real name.

She needed to tell him the truth. She had to. "Luke—" She took a second, waiting to see where she could start.

"I know."

She startled, staring at him intently. "You know?"

"This is hard." He stayed right where he was, so close, and she needed that. She needed him just where he was. "I've spent the last week and a bit telling myself we shouldn't do this, but you know what? I don't care anymore. I know you're leaving town. I know you're just here on vacation, or looking for someone, or whatever." The way he glossed over such a major event wasn't his fault—he had no way of knowing the importance of the quest that had brought her to Cape Hope. "And most of all"—his voice cracked a little—"I know that we have to be so careful with Stella."

Guilt was now a part of Ally, permanently burned into her soul.

"She already really likes you, and I don't want her getting hurt. We need to make sure she knows you're not going to be here forever."

Ally nodded, and ridiculous tears made her throat hurt. She refused to give in to them—not in front of Luke, anyway. "I don't want to hurt her."

"I know that." He smiled broadly. "Because you're a good person, Amy." And then, moving closer, so his nakedness pressed to hers, he added, "You're one of the best people I've ever known."

Her heart turned over in her chest.

"You've brought me back to life."

And rain began to fall as they made love one last time before he had to leave, to get home to Stella and the real world. Rain fell outside the window, but they were impervious to it, blissfully unaware of anything except the sensations that came from being in one another's arms.

SHE WOKE UP with a start in the middle of that night. The rain had stopped falling, but the wind was still bitterly cross, shaking the cottage with its intensity and knocking branches of the trees overhead against the walls and the roof so she feared for the damage that might be caused.

But it wasn't the storm that had woken her.

At least, not the storm that raged outside. It was the tempest of worry building in her chest, the raging cyclone that she couldn't hope to ignore for much longer.

She had to tell Luke the truth. She needed him to know why she was in Cape Hope. He needed to know her real name.

And the tears that had thickened in her chest earlier that day as they'd lain side by side in bed, before they'd made love one last time, began to fall from her eyes, gliding down her cheeks. She lifted her knees to her chest and cradled her head against them, sucking in shallow rasps of air.

She had to tell him.

How had she thought she wouldn't? She had to tell him. And she would.

But when?

Because as soon as she did, wasn't there a risk that it might change things between them? Oh, she had to take that risk, but couldn't she delay it, just a little while longer? At least until she knew what she was going to do with her dad?

Everything was jumbled up. The moral compass that had guided her all her life, a moral compass her mom had helped keep in place, felt knocked off balance.

She was lost, and she didn't know how to find her way back to herself.

THE NEXT TIME Ally saw Stella and Luke, she made a point of talking about her home in Wisconsin—a lot. The only thing she knew with certainty was that Stella couldn't become collateral damage in all this. She wouldn't risk the little girl getting hurt because Ally couldn't work out her life.

She talked about her friends and the house she grew up in, her job, the snow that would have blanketed the streets by now, the way she liked to curl up on her sofa with the newspaper and a hot coffee and watch as the snow drifted down.

Even as Luke and Ally wrestled an enormous fir tree into the house and settled it in its stand, and Stella hung decorations haphazardly and Ally and Luke sat on the sofa, side by side, barely touching, but with a heat humming between them that was its own unique brand of magic, and she thought how tempting it was to want to hold on to this with both hands—she didn't let herself even imagine what a future with Luke and Stella might be like.

She enjoyed the moment, she felt the magic of it, but she

braced herself to let all this fade away.

But the weekend drew to a close, and she didn't go back to Beauty Falls, and she didn't tell Luke the truth.

She didn't drop the ax on her time in Cape Hope or risk things changing for her and Luke. Christmas was only a week away, and it stood like a line in the sand, an invisible circle on the calendar that would signal the end of all this.

Christmas was a time for family, and she had no family here.

Nonetheless, she found herself spending more and more time with Stella and Luke, casually hanging out with them—as much to spend time with Stella as with Luke. They'd eat dinner together, Stella gaining confidence in the kitchen and learning to cook a few more elaborate meals, like pizza dough from scratch and a vegetable lasagna that she gave a tick of approval, describing it as "epic."

On the weekend before Christmas, Ally came over early on Saturday morning, not to help cook, but to let Luke cook for her the one meal he claimed to have mastered—pancakes.

"It's kind of our tradition," he'd explained, leaning in the window of Ally's car as she idled the engine, ready to head home the night before. "Stella sifts, and I cook."

Ally's heart had turned over because it didn't matter if the pancakes were like rubber; the idea of Luke and Stella cooking for her filled Ally with a kind of yearning that should have squealed danger—and did, only she'd become adept at ignoring it.

"Okay, butterfly. Time for the magic."

Stella grinned and nodded, lifting the whisk from the bowl with flourish. "Ready?"

Luke nodded sagely. "Okay."

Stella began to whisk with enthusiasm, so a little of the batter slopped out of the bowl onto the counter. Stella winced, and Luke shrugged.

"Don't worry about it. You can't make an omelet without cracking eggs."

"What?"

"It's an expression," Ally explained. "It means sometimes, to get something really good, you have to make a bit of a mess."

Stella grinned her agreement, though she still whisked with a little more caution.

The pan sizzled and, a moment later, Luke took the pot from Stella, scooping a bit of batter in as a test pancake.

The sound of a car pulling up outside had all three turning toward the windows.

"Uncle Jacob!" Stella squealed excitedly, jumping down off the stool she'd been using and moving toward the front door. Ally caught the briefest look of consternation on Luke's features before the man she'd met at the diner the other week strode into the room, this time wearing jeans and a shirt, his blond hair pushed back from his forehead.

"Hey." Jacob crossed the kitchen, holding a hand out to Luke, who shook it. "Pancakes?"

Luke turned back to the pan, his back straight, his shoulders squared. "Yeah."

"You're helping?" Jacob turned to Ally, a slight frown on his handsome features. He was like Jen, she thought, remembering the wedding photo that revealed a pretty young woman with a straight nose and sparkling eyes.

"I'm just an audience member today," Ally explained as Jacob's eyes casually skimmed over her with undisguised curiosity.

"You're welcome to join us," Luke prompted, turning to face Jacob.

"Nah, I've already eaten." She couldn't say why, but Ally's pulse began to run faster and a sense of apprehension swirled in her chest. "I just came to drop back your chainsaw."

"You finally get yours fixed?" It was a joke, teasing—Ally presumed there was a backstory to the chainsaw.

But Jacob didn't smile. "Yeah." He turned to Ally once more. "Nice to see you again. Amy James, wasn't it?"

A *frisson* of anxiety bolted down her spine. She smiled to cover it. "Yep."

"From Wisconsin?"

She nodded.

"Where in Wisconsin?" It was just a question—he was making conversation, that was all.

"Madison." She swallowed; it didn't help. Nerves trembled inside her. "Have you ever been?"

He moved his head from one side to the other. "I'd like to, though."

"You should." She smiled uncertainly, aware of the way Luke was watching them. "It's beautiful."

"I'll check it out." He turned back to Luke, all casual friendliness once more, so Ally wondered if she'd imagined the interest he'd shown in her location. "I'll see you at Mom's Thursday?"

"What's Thursday again?" Stella prompted.

"Christmas Eve Eve," Luke said with a smile that Jacob matched—Ally guessed they were reflecting on the same memory.

"When Grandma does the song?"

Another smile between the men. Ally wanted to ask about it, but she felt hyperconscious of being an outsider. *Christmas is a time for family.* They were family; she wasn't. She'd ask Luke later, when they were alone. Her tummy flipped at that—being alone with him, late at night, was just about her favorite thing ever.

"That's the one."

"Oh, yay!" Stella clapped her hands together, then pushed her glasses higher on the bridge of her nose as the rapid movement had them slipping down a bit. "Can you come, Amy?"

"Stella," Luke chastised, but kindly, an apologetic smile in Ally's direction. "You can't just invite people to Grandma's house."

"But Amy's not just 'people.' She's Amy."

Luke's and Ally's eyes met, and they were both very still, as the dangers they were surfing crashed against them. Regardless of the care they'd taken, it was impossible to insulate Stella from the separation that was coming.

Ally needed to squash that hope, to remind Stella—gently—that this wasn't permanent, but before she could do that, Jacob spoke. "Grandma's got it all planned, sweetie. Maybe Amy can come another time?"

Stella seemed satisfied with this, though she did pout a little in response, and Ally told herself she was glad Jacob had been able to handle things so deftly. Only she wasn't glad. She had a strange feeling that the other man didn't like her or didn't trust her. Was it just that he was resentful of someone taking Jen's place in their lives?

Or was it about her? Did he somehow realize that she was sitting on a secret, that she was here on a lie?

What was she doing? Guilt made her stomach roll, apprehension had her digging her nails into her palms in an attempt to stave off a panic attack.

Much later, when Stella had been sent to bed and they were alone, Luke playing guitar and Ally watching, falling a little more for him in a way that she wanted to ignore, he paused midstrum and fixed her with a serious look. "I'm sorry about Jacob." The words came out of nowhere.

He began to play again, a soulful song that was beautiful and enigmatic. Ally listened, watching him, admiring the play of Christmas lights across his face, the symmetry of his features, the toughness of his jaw, and the skilled movement of his fingers over the frets. Then, "He's a good guy, really. He just likes to worry about us. He's protective."

"You need protecting?" she prompted, wishing it weren't true. Wishing she wasn't lying to him.

"He's not used to the idea of me and someone else."

"Because you've been single since Jen," she said thoughtfully.

"Yeah."

"And he thinks you're always going to be?"

Luke shrugged. "Up until two weeks ago, I would have thought the same thing."

Ally was very still, her eyes running over Luke's face while a sense of panic rose within her. It was like driving at high speed down a one-way street and not being able to find the brakes or the exit.

They shouldn't be doing this.

The way he was talking should be reserved for someone special, someone who would mean something. He deserved a real relationship with someone who didn't have so many emotional hang-ups.

Ally was frozen still.

Luke noticed. "You think that's weird?"

"No." Her eyes were huge in her face. "I was just thinking how...unexpected this is. I mean, in some ways, you're so not like the guys I usually go for and, in others, you're completely my type."

"Now, that is interesting. In what ways am I different?"

"You're not a total loser, for a start."

He laughed softly and stood, moving to sit beside her on the sofa. The fire crackled in the grate behind them and, in the corner, the tree they'd picked out together and watched Stella decorate was glowing with a thousand bright little lights. "You like losers, huh?"

She thought about that. "I don't like them so much as gravitate toward them."

He lifted his arm up on the sofa, running it behind her. "And in what ways am I your type?"

Her smile was tinged with melancholy. "That's easy. You're unavailable."

His laugh was a short sound. "Really? As evidenced by the way I've been following you around like a puppy dog since you arrived in town? Or the way I've rolled out the welcome mat for you in my home?"

She laughed. "I mean, you're emotionally unavailable. Or you should have been. You were."

"Yeah, I was," he agreed. "Until I met you." He moved his hand off the sofa back to the base of her neck, his fingers so light they stirred goosebumps along her flesh. "So," he spoke into the silence. "Unavailable guys?"

She nodded.

"You like to torture yourself?"

Her smile was just a lopsided shift of her lips. "Apparently."

"I'm serious."

"So am I."

He smiled, leaning closer, and her breath became raspy and shallow. "You don't think you deserve a nice, non-loser, emotionally available guy?"

She bit down on her lip. "I think I like things to be uncomplicated," she said carefully and then searched for a better way to express what she meant. "I like to know when and why a relationship will end, even before it starts. If I'm with a jerk, it's easier to walk away."

His expression tightened and for the briefest moment she thought she saw anger in his eyes, but it was gone again just as quickly. "And if you're with a non-jerk?"

"You're probably the first one of those." She moved a hand to his thigh, running her fingers over it distractedly, frowning. "And we know when it will end, for different reasons." She angled her face to his, the smile dying on her lips when their eyes met and the air around them seemed to grow thick and heavy with awareness and need.

And even though she kept telling herself this was casual and temporary, she knew Luke now better than she knew just about anyone. So even as he leaned his head forward to buzz his lips over hers, she saw the little line between his brows and knew that he wanted to say something, to disagree with her, but was holding it back.

She was glad—it was far nicer to kiss than to argue.

Chapter Eleven

WALKING ALONG MAIN Street, Ally was completely lost in thought. So it wasn't until Stella tapped her on the waist that she realized the little girl was walking right beside her. "Oh!" She startled, smiling at Luke's daughter.

"Hey." Stella's bespectacled face was so sweet, Ally knew she wasn't just falling for Luke—there was this precious girl, too. A little girl who deserved a mother's love. If one good thing could come from this brief affair, it was the hope that she'd helped Luke heal enough to open his heart again. Not to Ally—but to someone more suited to him. Someone who lived here, who believed in the power of love and the promise of forever, someone who deserved him. And the hope that love could lead to a family for Stella.

"We're getting ice cream." She grinned.

"Ice cream? Today?" She gave an exaggerated shiver.

Stella giggled. "Yep. It's already cold, so why not?"

"I guess there's some kind of logic to that."

"Wanna come?"

Ally looked around for Luke instinctively.

"Not Daddy. Grandma." She pointed a gloved hand

down the street, and Ally saw a blonde woman walking toward them, a curious look on her features. She was very like Stella—the same little nose, and similar eyes, but with skin that had been stretched to accommodate a smile so often it had formed happy lines close to the eyes.

Nervousness surged inside Ally. "Your grandma?"

"Yeah. Come on." Stella's little hand wrapped around Ally's, and she pulled her toward "Grandma." Once they were closer, she let go. "Grandma, this is Amy."

Ally wanted the ground to open up and swallow her whole. She'd never imagined the ripples in the pond that one simple white lie could cause. She'd never anticipated any of this. Not meeting Luke, not falling for him, not becoming a part of his life, Stella's life, and now Jen's mother's…

"Oh, good! I've been looking forward to meeting you." The woman's smile was kind—there was no hint here of the suspicions her son had seemed to feel. Maybe Ally was overthinking that? Perhaps it was just his authoritative manner that made him seem a little unsure of her? "My granddaughter has told me so much about you."

Ally nodded, still wishing for that convenient hole in which to disappear.

"I'm Cynthia."

"Nice to meet you." She didn't want to say her fake name. She was sick of it. She was sick of all of this. And though it wasn't logical, she felt a renewed anger for her father then, blaming him—even when she knew this had been her choice alone.

"I've heard you're a wonderful chef," Cynthia commented, falling into step beside Ally. "Stella raves about your meals."

"She's a talented apprentice," Ally demurred.

"It's nice for her."

Stella skipped a little way ahead, looking in the windows as she went, all of which were adorned with festive decorations, shimmering with lights and merriment.

"Cooking?"

Cynthia's eyes were laced with meaning and emotion when she looked at Ally. "Having a woman around."

Ally's heart jerked hard. "Oh."

Cynthia sighed. "Luke was pretty cut up after…we lost Jen."

Ally's breath was tortured in her lungs. "Yeah." What else could she say?

"We all were." Cynthia lifted a hand and ran it over a simple chain she wore at her neck. "No mother expects to lose their child. And just like that." Her expression grew wistful, contemplative. "Jen was so excited about the baby. We didn't have a lot, you know, but we loved each other so much. She would have been an excellent mommy."

Pain lanced Ally's chest. "I'm sure."

"I wish I'd gotten to see that." Cynthia's expression was wistful. "Luke's done Jen proud, though. He's doing a fine job. But he's lonely. I've been worried about him."

God, Ally thought, desperately wishing she didn't feel like this. Desperately wishing everything was different. What had she done? These were real people, and she was lying to all of them. "He seems okay," Ally murmured, the words totally insufficient for what she wanted to offer. But she just felt like a big liar, and like she didn't deserve to give this woman any kind of comfort. "He's a good guy."

Cynthia's smile was knowing. "Yes, dear. He is."

"I lost my mom earlier this year," Ally was surprised to hear herself offer. "It was a surprise, too. She wasn't sick or anything. One day she was there, and the next she wasn't." They slowed, almost to a stop. "I know a little bit about what that does to you. That sudden, unexpected void that opens up right here." She pointed to her chest.

Cynthia nodded. "Yes, that's just what it's like." The older woman turned to look at Stella, who was outside the diner now, hopping from one foot to the other either in an attempt to get warm, or with the sheer force of her impatience. "You've been good for her."

Inwardly, Ally grimaced. "I haven't really done anything."

Cynthia shook her head a little to dismiss that. "You've made her smile. You've made Luke smile."

"I'm...just visiting," Ally said quickly. "I live in Wisconsin."

Cynthia scanned Ally's face. "We live where we choose to live." The sage words were delivered with a small smile. "But you and I both know life is too short for bad choices."

Ally's eyes flew wide at the woman's perceptiveness. She wanted to blurt out the truth, to stop her from being so darned kind to Ally. She didn't.

"Would you like to come have coffee with me while Stella chooses her ice cream?"

Ally wanted that. She really, really did. But she'd already dug a big enough hole for herself. It was time to stop play-acting and start cleaning up her mess. "Another time," she said with a shake of her head. "Say goodbye to Stella for me."

She spun around and moved quickly back down the street, unable to take another moment of kindness from anyone.

ALLY SUCKED IN a deep breath and waited out the front of the restaurant. It was early—way before opening time, but she hadn't been able to wait a moment longer. She'd gone home after her conversation with Cynthia, and her resolution had formed, so the only solution to her problems was staring her right in the face. She had to see her dad and tell him who she was. And then she had to tell Luke everything. She owed him that—come what may. He might be angry, but at least he'd know she respected him enough to be honest.

Four days before Christmas, and it was frigid and icy.

Every exhalation was a white cloud. She rubbed her gloved hands together and tried not to think about home and the snow that would be falling there. She loved her home, she loved the streets she knew like the back of her hand, but, without her mom, it would be so strange and empty.

She paced the porch while she waited, her eyes flickering to the still-dark interior of the diner, then to the street. In her experience, chefs usually arrived long before front-of-house staff, to begin their prep, turn the coffee machine on, and get the restaurant ready for the first patrons.

After what felt like a very long time, but was probably only ten minutes, a car began to drive up the road, headlights dimmed. Ally's nerves jangled all over the place. This was why she'd come to Cape Hope.

She'd needed to find him, and she had.

She kept her eyes trained on him as he stepped out of the car and made his way toward her. Even his walk was familiar, echoing inside her like the ghost of a memory.

"Good morning." He took the few steps brusquely. "You've been in here before?" His eyes hovered on her features. "We're not open yet, but you're welcome to wait inside where it's warm."

Being this close to him and having him not recognize her hurt. It hurt worse, just about, than anything she'd ever felt, even losing her mom. "I need to speak to you."

"To me?" He looked at her more carefully and she thought, for a second, he might know who she was, that he might recognize his own daughter. But he just smiled again, encouraging her to speak.

Anger nudged out hurt. “It won’t take long.”

“Okay, sure.”

With a hand that was shaking, she reached into her handbag. “I have something of yours, and I wondered if you could explain to me what it is and why I have it.”

“Yeah?”

Her fingertips curved around the envelope. She swallowed past her hesitation, waiting as a truck drove down the street then cut its engine near the bakery a few doors down, before shoving the envelope toward him.

He took it on autopilot, frowning as he looked at it. His eyes scanned the address on the front, and his fingertips began to shake in a way that caused her stomach to knot and her tears to fill her eyes. “Where did you get this?”

But he knew. She saw it in the pallor of his skin and the slump of his shoulders.

When he lifted his head, his own eyes were wet. “Ally?”

She swallowed hard and fast and when he lifted a hand to touch her—as though perhaps she weren’t real—she stepped backward, her expression hard. “Yes. Your daughter.” She jerked on the strap of her handbag, so glad to feel angry, so glad it had rallied to her aid when other emotions were at risk of making her more vulnerable.

“It’s really you,” he whispered, taking a step toward her, so she squared her shoulders and glared at him.

"I found that envelope a few months ago and saw the postmark."

He nodded, his eyes full of feelings. "I never thought I'd see you again."

"Well, you did a damned good job of making sure of that."

His face crumpled as though she'd slapped him. "I have so many questions. Why don't you come inside so we can talk properly—"

"I don't want to talk," she whispered, wrapping her arms around her body, feeling ice-cold but not because of the temperature so much as what she was doing. She'd imagined this moment for so long and, now she was here, she was just full of sadness. A pervasive, soul-sapping sadness. "I came here to see if I could ever forgive you—to see if you could say anything that would make this okay."

"I get it. You're mad at me."

"Mad at you?" She scoffed, shaking her head. "I'm a thousand types of mad at you, Dad." The form of address slipped out instinctively before she could bite it back.

He nodded, his body tense, his face lined. "I have thought of you every single day since I left, Ally."

"Damn it, don't lie to me," she whispered, dashing away her tears impatiently. "You moved across the country and started a new life for yourself. You forgot I existed."

"No," he interrupted harshly, his own anger there. "I tried to contact you. Your mother—"

"Don't talk to me about Mom," she demanded, her voice sharp with the force of her insistence on that score. "Do you have any idea how hard things were for her after you left? Do you have any idea how hard things were for me?" She sobbed, spinning to face the street, bracing her hands on the railing. "Do you have any idea how much I missed you?" The last was just a whisper into the still-dark sky.

"If it was even a fraction of how much I missed you, then a crippling amount."

"I don't buy it," she said simply. "You could have come to me at any point. You could have written. You could have sent a damn check or two to Mom to help with raising me. Instead, you ran out and never came back for her or me; I don't think you gave us a second thought."

"What do you think was in that envelope, Ally?"

She turned to face him, her jaw locked rigid as she scowled and waited for her father to expand.

"As soon as I was on my feet in any way, I sent checks. Often."

Disbelief flew through her. "I didn't know that."

"I was a mess when I was married to your mom. I was an alcoholic, hun." Her heart rolled. "I drank. I drank so much. Don't you remember that?"

"Yes," she snapped.

He sighed. "But you remember it as a child. You can't understand what it was like."

"I remember you drinking, and I remember you

fighting," she muttered, crossing her arms. "But everything was always fine afterward."

"No, it wasn't. It was never fine." He dug his hands into his pockets, his face lined with regrets. "I treated your mom in a way I'll be ashamed of for the rest of my life." He bent his head, his regret palpable. "I drank myself to oblivion almost every day. I lost my job because of alcoholism."

She refused to let this soften her toward him. "So? You could have gotten help…"

"Addiction isn't like that," he said urgently, moving closer. "I was a danger to you both."

"Don't rewrite the past," she pleaded. "You never hit Mom or me."

"No, I don't mean that." He dragged a hand through his hair, and she saw it was shaking, his own emotions apparently rioting through his system. "The night before I left Wisconsin, your mom and I fought."

"I remember." It had been close to Christmas, just like this. Out of nowhere, she remembered the feeling of the Jesus sculpture in the palm of her hands and the way she'd prayed and prayed for their fighting to stop. In some ways, her prayers had been answered.

He winced. "Did she tell you why?"

Ally narrowed her eyes. "Does it matter?"

"I got you from school that day. I picked you up and drove you home. Drunk. I don't mean a little drunk. I mean so drunk that I sideswiped two parked cars. And when we got home, I started cooking dinner, then passed out on the sofa while you played in your room. Your mom came home to the damaged car, the door wide open, the stove on fire, all a myriad of ways I could have killed you—my daughter—in one afternoon."

Ally's breath jammed in her windpipe.

"She was furious, and I was so drunk and so angry with her. I couldn't believe she was giving me a hard time. And then I left, to blow off steam, and I sobered up. And I realized how close I'd come to…to the worst thing that could happen. I couldn't trust myself to live with you anymore, Ally."

Her chest hurt, like she'd been hit in dodgeball. But she glared at him, holding on to her anger.

"I drank for a long time after I left you guys. I drank and I drank, and every time I hit rock bottom, I hit it again, deeper and harder, until I was floundering, my liver pickled, my brain scrambled, and you and your mom were like a mirage in my very distant memory. I couldn't have even said if you were real or not."

Pain sliced through her.

"I lived on the streets. I ate out of garbage cans. I wasn't fit to be anyone's dad."

Tears fell down Ally's cheeks.

"I hitchhiked my way out here about five years after I left you."

"God." She swept her eyes shut, needing to process this,

her tender heart instinctively warming with sympathy, but her hurt railed against that, shielding her from any kind of softening to this man.

"And a funny thing happened in Cape Hope."

"Yeah?" She narrowed her eyes, her chest splitting. "What's that?"

"I found hope." He grimaced, perhaps at the sweetness of the sentiment. "I ran out of money, and I squatted in a barn on the edge of a farm—I know it now as the Heyworth Estate. I reckon the owner knew I was there, but he turned a blind eye. I wasn't hurting anyone. I'd find food left just outside—fruit, milk, cheese, bread." He grimaced. "It was a small act of kindness, but it made all the difference to me. I started to see myself as a person again. It made me realize other people saw me as a man, not just a drunk."

"You were always more than a drunk to me," she said firmly. "You were my dad." The words rang with accusation.

"I know that." He shook his head with visible frustration. "Can't you see that only someone who loved you very much would leave you? I chose to walk away because that was best for you. And your mom."

Ally sucked in an uneven breath, her eyes sparking with two decades of feelings. "If you knew what I've gone through, you'd know how absurd that is."

"What do you mean?"

"It was selfish!" she shouted, and then took a small step backward. "It was so selfish, Dad," she tried again, softer.

"Staying would have been selfish. I was ruining your mom's life. I lived in fear of ruining yours. Of hurting you."

"You did hurt me."

Remorse was clear in his lined face. "But look at you, Ally. Look at the woman you've become." He gestured toward her, and she wished he could see, she wished he understood. For all that she might look strong and like she was doing okay, she wasn't.

"You don't get it," she whispered, haunted. "I have missed you *every day.* I have loved you *every day.* I've hated you, too. I've wanted you, looked out at the stars and wondered if you were even *alive.* My own dad." Tears filled her eyes.

"I've thought of you, too, believe me."

"I don't believe you," she spat. "You looked me in the eyes in the café the other day, and you didn't so much as flinch. You didn't recognize me. You didn't remember me."

His skin paled. "It's been twenty years and you're so different…"

"Yeah." She snorted. "That happens. I grew up." She took another step back. "And you weren't there."

"I wish I could have been." He dragged a hand through his hair. "God, Ally, I wish things had been different."

"So? What? Why? You're here now. Why didn't you come back? You're obviously doing well. You're not still drinking?"

"No." His eyes assumed a faraway expression. "By the

time I left Cape Hope, I knew I wanted to make a change. I set off for Beauty Falls late one night—no real idea where I was going, just that I felt like I wanted to walk in that direction—and somewhere along the way, Bishop Douglas pulled over, offered me a lift and a room. I'd decided to make a change, and here was my salvation."

There was a part of her that wanted—grudgingly—to commend him on that, but it all smarted too darned much.

"I worked so hard on getting sober, and in the back of my mind, you were there, Ally. No, not the back of my mind. You were right at the front. It wasn't easy. It was the second hardest thing I've ever done. But I needed to make a change; I knew that. I worked at it, and I slipped up a few times, but I always found my way back to sober living. I needed to be the kind of man you deserved as a dad. I got sober for you."

Ally's eyes swept shut, pain making her throat constrict. "But you were *nowhere.* Never, at any of the times I needed you, were you there for me." She swallowed, trying not to think about the time she'd broken her arm or when her first boyfriend had broken up with her a week before prom, or, six months ago, when she'd gotten the call that her mom had died. "You weren't there for me." It was just a whisper, but she might as well have shouted these words.

He flinched, and made a low groaning noise. "I wrote to your mom," he said after a tortured beat of silence. "As soon as I was back on my feet. I had a job and a paycheck. Things were looking up. I had friends and a community. I wrote her, Ally. I wanted to fix this."

Ally froze. He'd obviously written—she had an envelope to prove it—but she'd presumed it had been a one-off. Not that there'd been more than one letter. "When?"

"Once I was sober. Once I'd been sober long enough to believe it would stick. I wanted to come back. Not to your mom, but to you, Ally. I wanted to be in your life."

Her insides were awash with pain and hurt. "She never told me that."

"She only replied once," he said quietly. "About three years after I started to write. I kept asking for a photo of you—or a phone call. Anything. I wanted to find a way back into your life, but I knew I couldn't just turn up—I knew I'd given up any rights to know you years earlier."

Ally was very still, his words chasing around her mind so nothing else made any sense. "Did she send one?" She swallowed. "A photo, I mean."

His eyes narrowed, and for a moment Ally felt something like anger pulse through him. "No." He compressed his lips. "She replied that I could go to hell—with no idea I'd already been there and back. She wrote that you'd never forgive me nor would she."

Ally's heart rolled because she knew her mom had missed Jack, and her anger had never dimmed. "If you'd really wanted to be a part of my life, that wouldn't have stopped you."

"It didn't," he assured her with urgency. "I kept trying. Check the postmark on this." He lifted it. "It's from two years ago. I kept writing, I kept sending checks, I pleaded with her, Ally, again and again, and never heard back. My checks were cashed, so at least I knew she was getting them. I never thought I'd see you again, but it didn't matter. At least I was doing some small thing for you."

Her eyes shimmered with ferocity. "Not enough."

He swallowed. "What could I have done?"

"Not left!" She crossed her arms and tilted her face up to the sky, taking a second to calm her racing pulse. "You're my dad," she said finally. "And you left me." He nodded, but before he could speak, she cut him off. "There's nothing you can say to make this better," she murmured. "If I'd been separated from my child, I'd cross the fires of hell to get back to them."

"You have a child?"

"I'm speaking hypothetically." And from experience—she'd seen the way Luke was with Stella and knew that was how a father should love their kid.

"I didn't deserve you," he said quietly with a firmness that cut right through her soul. "I didn't deserve to be in your life." He took another step forward but made no effort to touch her. He simply looked, his eyes tracing the lines of her face.

"So you made a choice not to be?"

He shut his eyes for a moment, his pain apparent. "I ruined it. I had no right to expect that you'd forgive me."

"I have spent twenty years not knowing…not knowing if you're alive or dead…"

"I wanted you to know."

She bit down on her lip, fury and grief weakening her by degrees until she felt completely slumped over. She'd felt such rage at her father for his disappearing act, but if what he said was true—and the envelope she'd carried in her bag all the way from Wisconsin did seem to support his story—then her mom was at least partly to blame. Not for Jack's departure, but for keeping his life a secret from Ally. For keeping him away when Ally had wanted her dad with all her heart.

If Sasha were alive, Ally probably would've felt aggrieved. Angry. She would've confronted her mom and demanded answers. She couldn't do that, but nothing changed the fact that her mom had stood between Jack and Ally. And maybe Sasha had felt she had her reasons, just like Jack had thought he'd had his reasons for leaving Ally. They were both wrong.

Ally had grown up without a dad, and it hadn't been necessary.

Hurt and disappointment swirled through her. She just wanted the world to stop spinning; she wanted to run far, far away and hide herself from all of this.

Why had she come here?

"You've grown so much."

Ally crossed her arms over her chest. "It's been twenty years." Twenty years of wondering, twenty years of feeling like maybe she'd done something wrong, maybe she was the reason he'd left, twenty years of feeling unlovable. She shook her head, moving down the porch, toward the steps. "I came here wondering if you could say anything that would fix this, and you can't." Tears filled her eyes.

"Please don't go."

Her eyes sparkled with the irony of that, and he lifted his palms in silent acknowledgment.

"Stay. For breakfast. Tell me about yourself."

She laughed, but a deranged sound without humor. "No, Jack. You don't get that. You don't get to know me now." She was trembling, freezing and emotional and so angry. "Do you get that I have spent almost my whole life missing you? That you left me and it changed who I am?" Her voice cracked a little. "I wanted to see you, I needed some kind of closure, but now it's over. Go back to pretending I don't exist."

"I never did that! Ask your mom, Ally. Speak to her—she'll tell you that I wrote, often. That I called, and she hung up on me. That she changed your number." Ally *did* remember that. At least three times, their number had been changed, and Ally had had to give out new numbers to her friends. "I kept hoping you'd answer. You never did. I wanted to be a part of your life once I knew I'd gotten myself together again."

"I don't care," she lied. "And Mom died this year," she whispered, looking away with her jaw locked to stop the monumental sob bubbling up inside of her from bursting forth.

"I'm sorry." He dragged his palm over his jaw. "I didn't know that."

"Why would you? You weren't a part of our lives. She was just some woman you used to be married to."

He didn't respond at first. Then quietly, with the appearance of calm and a gentle, conciliatory tone, "You're freezing. Come inside. Have a coffee to warm you up."

"I don't need a damn coffee." She stood on the top of the steps and looked at Jack Monroe, committing his face to memory as it was now, to write over the top of the far-away, long-ago recollections that haunted her.

"I came to a point where I presumed you'd forgotten me."

"You're my dad." So simple. So soft. So achingly heartfelt.

"And you're my little girl, even though you're all grown up now. Come inside, please. Let me talk with you. Or have dinner with me tonight. Something—anything. Just a start, Ally. I want to know about you. I want to…fix this."

The words were swallowed up by her certainty that this was beyond repair. "No. This isn't about what you want. You don't have any say in this. *I* wanted to see you, and now I have, and I know it was a mistake to come looking for you. You're not my dad anymore. You're no one to me." Tears wet those words, but she spun blindly, stalking down the steps and onto the sidewalk.

He followed. “Don’t leave like this, please.”

She scoffed. “You’re the expert in leaving.”

“Yeah, I am. What I did was a truly awful thing, but I was putting your life in danger, all the time. I didn’t deserve you.”

“So say that. Go to rehab. Get fixed. But come back. You don’t walk out on someone for almost their entire life and expect it to be okay.”

“I don’t expect it to be okay.” He stopped as she reached her car. “I just want to know about my daughter.”

Her eyes fixed him with a glare as she yanked open the driver’s-side door. “It’s too late for that. It’s too late for any of this.”

“If you really believed that, you wouldn’t have come.”

Pain lanced through her, because he was right, but it was too much. She was on overload. “I can’t do this.” She sat in the car and started the engine, staring straight ahead so she didn’t have to look at him again. This whole idea had been a disaster.

She closed her eyes for a second and saw her home in Wisconsin and knew she had to go back. To get away from her dad, from this, from everything that reminded her of him. She had to go home and forget she’d ever come. This had been a mistake, and the sooner she left, the better.

She tried not to think about Luke.

It hurt too much, and she was already hurting enough.

Besides, she'd lied to him and, once he knew, he wouldn't want her anymore. Just like her dad hadn't wanted her.

She banged her palm into the steering wheel and pulled onto the road, pointing the car in the direction of Cape Hope and refusing to look in her rearview mirror. It didn't matter if Jack was watching her drive off or not. She didn't care. He was in her past and he was going to stay there from now on.

"LISTEN TO ME, buddy." Jacob was talking quietly to make sure Stella didn't overhear. Not much chance of that—she had her earphones on and was dancing away to the latest JoJo song, going by the accompanying high-pitched warble. Outside, early morning rain hammered the earth, creating puddles in the ground. "She's not there."

"What are you talking about?" Luke passed a coffee mug over, propping his hip on the counter as he waited for his brother-in-law to expand.

"I found one Amy James in Madison, Wisconsin, whose date of birth would fit your friend's. She looks completely different. Whoever that woman is you've been cooking with and whatever"—he said the word with disapproval—"she's not who you think."

Luke's chest cracked a little, but he was sure his friend

had got it wrong. Thunder clapped in the distance, and he remembered the way Amy had been afraid of the storm that day in the cottage, when he'd gone to patch the roof and found himself clicking together in a new and different way, all because of Amy. Uneasiness shifted in his gut, but he refused to acknowledge it. "Why are you running background checks on her?"

A hint of guilt flexed the muscles around Jacob's eyes. "You're spending a lot of time with her." He shrugged.

"I told you it wasn't serious. She's leaving soon." The words filled his mouth with bitterness. Suddenly he thought about Christmas without Amy and the world no longer made sense. Panic filled him, panic from a thousand different directions.

"You're missing my point." Jacob rounded back on their conversation. "This woman is lying to you."

Instinctively, Luke rejected that. "You must have spelled it wrong."

Jacob refuted it. "I spelled it every way there is."

Luke shook his head. It didn't make sense. Nothing about this made sense anymore, but he trusted Amy, trusted her completely. "She wouldn't lie to me."

"She has. There's no such person as Amy James from Madison, Wisconsin, at least not who looks like your Amy. Whoever you're spending time with, you don't even know her name."

Luke ran his fingers through his hair, pulling at its ends

distractedly. "I can't...why would she use a fake name?"

"In my experience, never for any good reason."

Luke's brows shot up. "You're actually suggesting she might be a criminal? On the run from some kind of cooking heist?"

"This isn't a joke." Jacob's voice was firm. "Has she given you any reason to think she's hiding something from you?"

Luke thought back to their time together—and they'd spent a *lot* of time together since they'd met. It had been kind of a whirlwind affair. He turned his head slowly, rubbing a hand over his chin, his eyes holding his brother-in-law's. He thought about the sense he occasionally had that she was holding something back, that she was keeping something from him. And maybe she was. Maybe there were things in her life she hadn't shared with him, but nothing like this. He couldn't say how he knew, but he did. "I trust her."

"Fine. Maybe I'm wrong," Jacob offered in a way that showed he didn't believe it for one minute. "Talk to her. Ask her."

Luke frowned. It didn't make any sense. "I just don't see why...I mean, *why* would she lie about something like her name?"

"I don't know." Jacob flicked a glance over his shoulder to where Stella was dancing enthusiastically, waving her hands in the air as she spun around. "But you should probably find out. For Stella's sake."

Chapter Twelve

SHE DROVE TO Cardinal Cottage on autopilot, the path now somehow interwoven in her DNA so she was convinced she could find the way blindfolded. And as she drove, she replayed the conversation with her father, even when she wanted to blot it out, to forget about it, to forget about him.

"You're my little girl, even though you're all grown up now."

She sobbed into the emptiness of her car, the tears on her face falling as frantically as the torrential rainwater that lashed the car.

"I came to a point where I presumed you'd forgotten me."

She banged her hands on the steering wheel, turning the car toward Cardinal Cottage, up the drive, barely able to see now. But even in the pouring rain, with eyes that were loaded with salty tears, she recognized the red pickup by the front door of the cottage and she moaned, because she was both desperate to see—and terrified of seeing—Luke Miller. Yet here he was, like somehow he knew she needed him.

She pulled her Prius to a stop, but before she cut the engine, he was out of his car, his low-slung jeans and plaid shirt with the leather jacket over the top all getting saturated, so by the time he reached her door he was wet through. He opened it, staring down at her, and his expression was unlike anything she'd seen before. It was storm clouds and thunder-claps.

"Luke?" Her heart backflipped, hard. Something was wrong. She immediately thought of Stella, and concern weakened her knees. "What is it?"

He took a step back from the car, rain making his hair form a pelt on his head. She stared up at him, waiting for him to answer, her breath held, her mind jolting into a different gear now. "Who are you?"

She stopped dead in her tracks. The three words were the last thing she expected. "What do you mean?"

He looked toward the sky for a second, as though fortifying himself, and then with a guttural sound to his voice said, "Are you Amy James?"

Her gut rolled. Guilt made her throat burn. "What…I…"

"Tell me the truth." The words rumbled from deep in his chest.

But her silence, surrounded by the rain and the thunder, spoke volumes.

His gruff laugh lacked humor; it was laced with disbelief. "You're not, are you?"

She sucked in a breath as she pushed out of the car, unable to find words, so she just gaped, staring at him, needing him to understand with no idea how to make him.

"Jesus!" The word flew from his lips, his anger palpable. "What the hell is going on?"

"I..."

"Who are you?" He pushed a hand through his wet hair. In the distance, lightning sliced the gray fabric of the sky, and she trembled, but fear of the storm was way down on her list of feelings now.

Luke had become collateral damage even when she'd wanted to avoid that. She should have told him. It didn't matter that she'd planned to—she'd left it too late. "I'm the same woman you've been getting to know," she promised, and it was true.

"Getting to know," he snapped with disbelief. "I don't even *know* your name."

She swallowed, breathing almost impossible. "It's Alicia Monroe—Ally."

He closed his eyes, like maybe he'd been hoping he was wrong, right up to that moment.

"How did you find out?" The words were too soft, the storm too loud.

"What?"

"I said, how did you find out?" she shouted so he'd hear her.

"That you're not Amy James?" He moved closer, his eyes swirling with disbelief as they scanned her face, like he was looking for a relic of the woman he'd been spending time with. "Does it really matter?"

She was trembling, but not from cold. Just like earlier that morning, out the front of Cup of Joe, she'd been cold in an almost otherworldly kind of way, like her bones had slowly turned to ice.

"Damn it, Amy—whoever you are—I need you to start being straight with me. Christ! I've invited you into my life, my dauther's life, my home, and I don't know anything about you!"

"You do know me," she whispered, tears filling her eyes. Then, louder, "You know everything about me except my name." Rain was stinging her eyes as it fell, but neither of them moved; neither of them sought shelter. It was like this conversation was bigger than either of them, bigger than such a rudimentary concern as the weather.

"Why? Why have you been calling yourself something different? What is this?"

"I didn't plan to meet you." She groaned, wrapping her arms around her torso, her hair plastered to her head. "I didn't plan to get to know anyone while I was here."

"Why not?" he demanded, a step closer now so they were toe-to-toe.

The truth was there, like a flicker of flame in the midst of this storm, the flicker she'd acknowledged she would need to tell him days ago – and even before that. She'd hated lying to him. She closed her eyes, sucking in an icy-cold breath before speaking slowly, calmly, even when her insides were being squeezed and stretched. "I didn't come to Cape Hope to find some long-lost friend of my mom's."

The air around them crackled with silence while the rain fell and the sky rolled with thunder—suspicion and betrayal arced in his face, and her heart broke for him, because he'd been alone for six years, and then he'd trusted her, he'd let her in. No wonder he was so furious. She hated that he was angry and with her—and that he had every reason to be. "So you lied about that, too?"

His scathing indictment hurt, most of all because there was a kernel of truth in it. And even though she'd had damned good reasons for lying, she suspected Luke was someone who dealt in black and white, good and bad, right and wrong. His brand of morality wouldn't accept the existence of a reasonable lie. "Jack Monroe isn't just some friend of my mother's," she tried for more precision.

He waited, but not patiently. She saw his expression shifting and changing, and her heart broke. She wanted to drop her head to his chest and wrap her arms around his waist. She needed him to comfort her. She needed him. Her heart was already too hurt, battle-wearied by the morning she'd had, and Luke was the only person who could make that feel better. She wanted to ask him to do that, but she couldn't. She wouldn't.

She was on her own in this, just like everything else.

"He's my dad, Luke." Her voice cracked. "Jack Monroe is my dad, and I had no idea where he was. That was all true." She took a breath, searching for words. "All my life, since he left, I've wondered. I thought he'd just dropped off the face of the earth. Then Mom died, and I found an envelope with his handwriting on it and a postmark from Cape Hope. And for no reason except that I have always wanted to know—needed to know—why he left me, I set off here. Hoping to find him." A sob bubbled out of her. "I thought if I could see him, I'd finally understand why he left me, and I wouldn't have to spend the rest of my life feeling like we just weren't enough for him. Like *I* wasn't enough."

Like I wasn't worthy of his love.

Some of her words got swallowed up in the storm but not all of them. Luke stayed immobile, but watchful, his expression showing he was listening intently.

"I came to Cape Hope looking for my dad, and none of this"—she gestured from him to her, her fingertips brushing his chest—"was meant to happen."

A muscle jerked in his strong, square jaw and her tummy flip-flopped again and again. "So why didn't you tell me this? Why did you have to use a fake name?"

Her eyes swept shut. "I didn't want him to know I was here until I was ready to talk to him."

"You thought I'd, what? Tell someone? You didn't trust me?" His hurt was palpable.

She inhaled sharply, shaking her head. "I met a lot of people when I came here. It wasn't about you, specifically," she said honestly, grimacing. "I don't mean you weren't important, that you didn't come to mean more to me, but you and I…this…is separate from why I came to Cape Hope." She swallowed, her throat raw.

"I could have helped you. I would have wanted to help you." He had to shout to be heard over the rain.

His kindness was something she should've known to expect, but it hurt, because she hadn't, and it caught her completely unawares. "I didn't want you to know." Her eyes met his, and she felt something slip into place; a comprehension she'd been dancing around firmed up. "I didn't want you to see me like this."

"Like what?" he demanded.

She forced herself to say it aloud, something her subconscious had been thinking a long time. "Broken. Weak."

Her words were like a storm cloud between them. "Jesus, Ally." He dragged a hand through his hair. "Because you wanted to find your dad?"

She bent her head, pain lancing her gut. She nodded, knowing how vulnerable she must seem and hating that.

"Do you think it would have changed a damn thing for me?"

"I don't know." The words came out so soft, there was no way he could have heard them. It didn't matter. None of this mattered.

"He hurt you. He did something incomprehensible. That's a reflection on *him*. Not you."

She understood what he was saying, but it did nothing to heal the hole in her heart. She looked away from him, angling her face toward the house.

"The fact you came looking for him shows how strong you are. Not weak. Not broken."

She sobbed, pressing the palms of her hands to her eyes. "I wanted to tell you. I nearly did, so many times, but I just had to do this first."

He angled his face away from hers, his eyes focused on the drive, his disbelief and rejection of that evident in every line of his face.

"How did you find out?" She came back to her earlier question.

"Jacob."

Ally's heart trembled. "He knows?" She thought back to the way he'd looked at her, to the suspicion she felt emanating off him in waves.

"He's protective," he said quietly. "He looked into you."

She nodded, jerking her head. "I get it. I'm glad. That you have someone like that." But she couldn't bear the distance any longer, and it had nothing to do with her needing comfort. She needed to comfort him, to make him understand that her not being honest with him was only a small part of what they were. "I'm so sorry I lied to you." She pressed her hand to his chest, needing him to feel the truth of that.

He turned back to face her, their eyes locked, rain falling hard and fast around them. "I know." The words were dragged from deep inside of him, and her heart turned over in her chest.

"I didn't mean to. It seemed so harmless when I first arrived." At this, his jaw clenched; she resisted an urge to lift up onto her tiptoes and kiss the muscle that was jerking there. "I didn't think I'd say more than two words to anyone. I didn't get how places like this work. I didn't know what kindness and friendliness I'd find—everywhere I looked. I didn't know I'd meet you, and Stella. I didn't know that I'd find my way into a family—into your family." She swallowed hard and fast, tears making it almost impossible to speak, but she needed to say this, to tell him how she was feeling.

"You didn't just lie once, Amy—Ally." His eyes were a darker shade than normal, his lashes made thick and clumpy by the rain. "You lied every minute we were together. Every laugh. Every story. Every kiss." His expression shifted. "You made a choice to keep lying to me even when I was opening myself up to you completely—opening my home."

She was glad it was raining, glad he wouldn't see how fast tears were falling from her eyes. "I wanted to tell you."

He took a step back then, his face stretched with the strength of his emotions. "Then you would have told me."

"It's hard," she said, her temper snapping. "It's hard, okay? By the time I realized you were someone I wanted to be honest with, we were so deep into this, and I had no idea if it would change how you felt about me. I didn't want to ruin anything. I didn't want to ruin this."

He glared at her for several beats, and her heart pumped hard and fast, so her blood seemed to explode in her veins. "Did you honestly think there was any way your lying to me about who you are and why you're here *wouldn't* ruin this?"

She froze, so still, so very still, while his words sank in.

"You were lying to me," he said, fixing her with a steady, impaling glare. "And I was opening myself up to the first woman I've been with since my wife died."

His words made her feel about two inches tall. "I'm so sorry, Luke." It wasn't enough. It was nowhere near enough. "I didn't mean for this to happen." She let out a small sob.

"I know that." He didn't shift; his face didn't change.

"It all happened so fast. We kept saying this was temporary. I never meant for it to get so serious between us."

He shifted his face, looking away again. "It's not serious," he said, after several long, rain-filled seconds.

She felt like she'd been pushed off a cliff. "It's not?"

"How can it be?" He stubbed his toe into the wet gravel underfoot. "You didn't even trust me enough to tell me why you were here." His face showed stubborn determination. "You didn't trust me enough to say, 'Hey, Luke, I need to be honest with you about something important, and I know it's weird that I lied, but if I tell you now, I think you'll understand.'" He let those words sink in. "You didn't trust me enough to think I would understand."

"I was going to tell you. I swear, Luke, this morning. I wanted to see him first, and then to come to you…"

He was very still, like he was processing that. "The problem with having lied is that it makes it hard to believe anything you say."

"Whoa." She took a step back, his words slicing through her like a knife might butter. "That's not fair."

"You know what's not fair?"

She shook her head.

"I honestly thought that, just maybe, I was falling in love with you." He stared at her, waiting for the words to digest.

Ally heard them, and her heart bounced around in her chest, because as soon as he said that, she knew she hadn't just been lying to him, but to herself as well. She didn't want to love Luke, but how could she not? How come she hadn't realized what had been happening between them? "Maybe you were," she whispered throatily, bravely, given how bashed her soul was.

"No." His eyes were hard. "This isn't love." He crossed his arms over his chest, his expression like granite. "This is a lie."

She sucked in a breath, thinking it couldn't get worse than this.

"This was a mistake."

"No, it wasn't." She fought that with every cell in her body. "Not for me."

He didn't say anything, but his chest moved up and down with the violence of his breathing.

"I have a habit of getting involved with guys who aren't

right for me. I like knowing relationships aren't serious. But everything about this was the opposite. This has been so right, Luke. I thought the fact I'm only in town on vacation would mean neither of us would come to care for each other, but jeez, was I wrong."

He still didn't speak. She had to be brave. She'd faced her demons once that morning, and she'd do it again, because she couldn't lose Luke. Not when she realized now how she felt for him. "You're the first guy I've been with that I've dreaded walking away from. Usually I'm looking for an exit, but with you, I just want more." She couldn't bear being apart from him a second longer. She moved closer, pressing a hand to his cheek, needing him to understand. "Not just you. Stella, too. I came here to find my dad, and instead I found you and Stella, and I fell completely in love with both of you." The second she said the words, she knew how true and right they were. They burst through her, body and soul; they fired inside of her. "I don't think this was a mistake," she said seriously. "And I think you know that I'm not a liar."

He stared down at her, and for once she had no idea what he was thinking. She swallowed, her nerves tighter than an overstretched rubber band, waiting for him to offer her something, anything. Waiting to see that he understood. "You don't love me."

She shook her head, preparing to deny that, but he kept speaking.

"If you loved me, you wouldn't have been able to keep lying to me. It would've killed you to share my secrets and keep all yours wrapped up tight in here." He pressed his fingers gently to her chest. "If you loved me, you'd know that trust is one of the things that matters most to me. Trust kept me alive in Iraq, having to lean on my unit, having to depend on my guys. You don't trust me, and you should know I'd never be able to trust you again."

She felt as though he'd punched her. She opened her mouth, but no words came to her.

"And I'd never love someone I didn't trust." He took a step away from her, his eyes sweeping over her figure, his expression grim. "I think it's a good thing you're leaving Cape Hope." He swung around, stalking toward his pickup.

But Ally wasn't done. She couldn't let him walk out on her without a fight—she wasn't going to lose someone else she loved. "Damn it, Luke." She ran after him, grabbing for his arm, pulling on it. He was big and strong, so it was by his choice that he turned to face her. "Damn it," she said again, crying openly now. "I made a mistake, but I swear to you, I was going to fix this. I was going to tell you the truth. If you knew what I'd been through today, and how much I need you, you'd listen to me. Please listen to me."

He was very still, his eyes glinting in his oh-so-heartbreakingly-handsome face. "I *would* have listened to you." He let the words sit between them a moment. "If you'd told me this, I would have listened, and I would have understood. If I'd heard it from you, rather than someone else, I would have tried to make sense of it. But I only have your word that you were ever going to have this conversation with me, and to be honest, your word doesn't really mean that much right now."

She drew in a ragged breath, his statement like acid against her flesh. "Luke..."

"This isn't love," he said finally. "And I know, because I've been in love, and it felt nothing like this."

Chapter Thirteen

IT STARTED TO snow just outside of Cleveland. Ally had been driving for hours by then, and she pulled into a diner to take a break, numb as she ordered a coffee and bagel, numb as she paid for it, numb as she walked back to her car, numb as she opened the door and saw her suitcase in the back seat, proof that she'd left Cape Hope, proof that she was going home.

Numb as she leaned against the car, her eyes shut for a second, remembering the look on his face as he'd told her this had been a mistake. That he'd thought he was falling for her, but he'd been wrong, because he could never love a liar.

He didn't love her.

And it wasn't until he'd said as much that Ally had realized how much she loved him. How hard she'd fallen for him and how desperately she'd needed him to feel the same.

But he didn't. He'd made that abundantly clear and there was nothing for it now but for Ally to leave town and try to forget about him. About them, because she'd fallen in love with Stella too.

She drove out of Cleveland, past buildings she'd seen

weeks earlier on her way to North Carolina. Only then, her mind had been full of thoughts of her dad, memories of her childhood, questions about his motivations and reasons for leaving her. Now, as the snow drifted over the road and everything looked so festive and beautiful, she felt the most profound, wrenching sadness.

He didn't trust her.

He didn't love her.

He didn't want her.

All her life she'd dealt with these feelings. She'd protected herself from getting close to anyone, because she'd wanted to avoid hurting like this again, and somehow, in the place she'd gone to in the hope of healing, she'd found her way to fresh hurt, new pain, enormous loss.

She'd gone to Cape Hope half broken. Broken by the loss of her mom, broken by decades of living with her father's desertion, and then, she'd started to feel whole again. She'd found herself in Luke's arms.

And yet…

He hadn't loved her. He didn't love her. He never would love her.

She was no longer half broken. She was done. Completely and utterly spent.

Ally drove on, and night fell, darknsess, stars, and wintry snow on either side of the car. As she prepared to take the exit for home, something bright in the sky caught her attention. She slowed down, her eyes following the light, the trajectory of the shooting star beautiful and mesmerizing all at once. It went past her Prius, slicing through the night sky effortlessly—as though it were a ballerina on stage performing a perfect pirouette—and she watched it with her breath held, all the while refusing to pay any heed to the fact it was traveling further away from her, lighting a path all the way to Cape Hope.

"YOU'RE NOT SMILING, Daddy."

Luke flicked his eyes to Stella's in the rearview mirror, making an effort to flash a grin across his features. It felt strange. Foreign. Just like it had for the last three days, since they'd argued and he'd driven away from Cardinal Cottage. Stella's glasses had slipped down a little on the bridge of her nose, and she adjusted them as he watched—a force of habit now, one she did so often he was pretty sure she didn't even realize it. "I'm driving."

"Yeah, but you usually smile when you drive."

He turned his attention back to the road, his grip unintentionally tight on the steering wheel. He stayed silent. He wasn't sure if he usually smiled or not when he was driving, but he did know he'd spent the last few days feeling like he'd been hit by a Mack truck at full speed.

"And you didn't smile when Grandma sang 'O Holy Night,' either."

"Why would I smile?"

"Cause of how she sings it."

"She forgets all the lyrics."

"Exactly," Stella said with a determined blink that reminded him so much of Jen his gut twisted. "And you always laugh when Grandma forgets the words to songs."

Spending the night with Jen's family had brought too many memories to the forefront of his mind. Memories of when she was just the kid sister of his best friend, memories of when she'd become more than that—when he'd started to go to Jacob's place hoping to catch a glimpse of Jen, when they'd first kissed, when he'd asked her to prom and when he'd proposed. He loved spending time over at their place, but her absence was so much more noticeable. And this year, there'd been guilt, too. Guilt because he was missing Jen but nowhere near like normal.

He was missing her, but he was thinking of Ally, wondering about her, wanting to talk to her, needing to see her. Wishing they hadn't argued. Wishing he hadn't told her he didn't trust her. Wishing he'd let her explain. Wishing he hadn't acted out of anger, because no matter what she'd done, she didn't deserve that.

He made a low groaning noise that had Stella's eyes narrowing in the mirror.

Ally had needed him. Flashes of their argument came to him, and for the first time in days, he put aside the mood he'd been in and paid attention to his memories of that morning. When she'd pulled up, he'd gone to the car, and she'd looked up at him and her face had been tear-streaked. Already. She'd been crying in the car.

What had she said? She'd wanted to tell him, but she'd wanted to see her dad first? That morning…

His gut felt like a rock had been dropped right through it.

Crap.

She'd seen her dad that morning. And she'd needed Luke to be there for her and, instead, he'd berated her for lying. She'd told him she loved him and had begged him to listen to her, and he'd clung to his anger because it had felt like what he needed to do.

He'd loved Jen. She'd been his wife. And Ally had lied to him. Had he been a bit relieved to have a reason to end it? Because that would mean he was somehow still faithful to Jen?

He stopped driving, pulling the car over to the side of the road and staring straight ahead.

"Daddy?" Stella's voice sounded miles away.

He'd looked around his mother-in-law's dining table and had seen everything through new eyes. It had been a good night, like always, even if Luke had felt like a bear with a sore head. Good food, music, Christmas everywhere he looked. Jen had been there in spirit—from the photos of her on the walls to the stories they'd shared, her own life inextricably bound to all of theirs. She'd been in the tears that had glistened in Cynthia's eyes as she'd given Stella a pin with a little pearl in its center—a piece of jewelry Jen had worn once, a long time ago. Jen was there, but life was going on without her; even her family was moving forward. Missing her like hell, and they always would, but still living their lives.

And he wasn't.

Comprehension was like a bolt of lightning jolting his brain. He *hadn't* been living his life. Not since she'd died. He'd poured all of himself into Stella, but he'd shut himself off to everything else, because he felt like he owed that to Jen—like that was how he should serve her or honor her or something.

And now he'd pushed Ally away because it was easier to be angry than it was to dig deep and forgive. To let her explain and understand what she'd been trying to tell him. She hadn't meant to lie. She hadn't meant to meet him. She'd wanted to be honest with him.

His fingers gripped the steering wheel hard.

That feeling he'd been hit by a truck wasn't an accident. It was his body's way of jerking his mind to attention, of telling him he'd messed up. He'd made a monumental mistake in letting Ally go when he should have fought for this, for them.

He swore softly under his breath and, from the back seat, Stella gasped. "Swear jar, Daddy."

"Sorry, honey." He gripped the wheel and spun the car

around carefully, pointing it back in the direction from which they'd just come. He'd been living his life asleep for too long, but now he had every reason in the world to wake up.

"Where are we going?"

"Cardinal Cottage." He turned the radio up to deter any more questions and drove with the devil at his heels.

He knew, though, the second he turned off the road and onto the drive that it was too late. Everything was dark. Pitch black.

Crap.

He stopped the car anyway. "Stay here." He slammed his door shut and jogged to the cottage. It was snowing and cold. He didn't care. He banged on the door and waited, then ran to the kitchen window. His gut rolled as memories slammed into him. The soup. Her smile.

The way she'd smoked the place up lighting a fire.

The first time they'd made love. His eyes lifted unconsciously to the bedroom window upstairs, and a visceral ache made his body tighten.

The fact she was gone made everything clear to him in a way nothing else could. He'd ruined it, and he'd lost her. She'd left and, worse than that, she'd left thinking he didn't trust her, didn't love her. She'd left, and it was completely his fault.

He jogged back to the car, with no idea if he could ever fix this but knowing he'd sooner die trying than give up.

"Stella, how would you feel about Uncle Jacob sleeping over tonight? There's something I need to take care of."

SNOW CAUSED DELAYS to his flights, so it was midmorning on Christmas Eve by the time he touched down in Wisconsin, and by then he realized he had no way of knowing if Ally would even be at home or not. Thanks to Jacob's police database, he had her address—though he didn't much like to think about the ethical implications of that. Desperate times had called for desperate measures, and he hadn't been about to hear no for an answer from his brother-in-law.

He took Jacob's cooperation as tacit approval for all this.

If she wasn't at home, then he'd wait. He looked out of the cab window at the falling snow, uncaring if that meant getting covered in the stuff.

The car cut through Madison, moving through an industrial-looking area that eventually gave way to a series of small but sweet cottages bounded by lawn—lawns that were covered in thick white snow now. Christmas wreaths hung on each door except one and, as the car slowed to a stop out the front, his heart sank.

Ally loved Christmas, but she hadn't even hung her own wreath out.

He paid cash for the cab and stepped out, sending a cursory glance up and down the street before crossing and taking the few steps to her porch in one stride. There was a buzzer, but when he pressed it, no noise sounded, so he banged on the door instead.

Nothing.

No footsteps. No noise whatsoever.

He took a step back, frowning, scanning the house for signs of life. There were no lights, no open blinds. It was all closed up. With a sinking feeling, he stepped backward further, looking for a gate he could use to check the back.

There was one, but closer inspection showed it was padlocked.

So then, he would wait, and he'd keep waiting, as long as it took.

SHE'D BARELY SLEPT since she got back to Wisconsin, but for the first time in days, Ally had found her way to a deep, if somewhat disturbed slumber. She was woken up to a banging sound that made it impossible to orient herself. It took her a moment to realize it was the middle of the day, and that she was back home. Not in Cardinal Cottage, not near Luke and Stella, not near her father.

She lay in bed a moment longer, staring at the white wall across from her, wishing whoever was knocking so loudly would go away. At this time of year, it was bound to be carolers or door knockers.

No one she knew.

Her chest groaned a little. She had friends. Not close friends, but friends. Only most of them were caught up with their families or traveling overseas. There was no one here in Madison for Ally. There was no one to see, nothing to do, no one who'd missed her or wanted to see her.

She swallowed past the lump in her throat, trying not to think of how alone she was, trying not to think of Luke and Stella and that cozy-as-all-get-out kitchen of theirs. Trying not to think of how, just for a moment, she'd felt like she actually belonged somewhere.

Another bang on her door, louder now. With a growl of impatience, she pushed out of bed, keeping the quilt her mom had made wrapped around her shoulders as she padded through the dark house—it was a gloomy day, and she'd kept the blinds drawn in the hope it'd help her get some rest—to the front door, yanking it inward.

Only to see the man who'd taken over her mind, body, and soul from almost the first moment they'd met.

Luke from Cape Hope, here, in Wisconsin. Luke, wearing those faded denim jeans and his leather jacket, looking every bit the sexy single dad Marine he was, so completely masculine and handsome all at once.

Luke standing there so devastatingly handsome, just the way he'd been when he'd looked her in the eyes and told her he didn't trust her and couldn't love her. "Mind if I come in?"

Nothing made any kind of sense. Instinctively she wrapped the blanket more tightly around her.

It had only been four days since she'd left Cape Hope and yet Ally stared at Luke as though it had been months. "What are you doing here?"

He shifted his weight from one foot to the other, jabbing his hands into his pockets. "I went to Cardinal Cottage. You were gone."

She swallowed, hurt so raw in her chest it was easy to summon it, to use it to protect her. "Yeah. You said you were glad I was going."

His face paled. "I remember."

She bit down on her lower lip. "I was always going to come home."

His expression shifted, his gaze piercing hers. "Were you?"

"That's what we said," she reminded him, shivering, her tone defensive.

He ground his teeth. "I know."

And then, the pain was too strong; it slashed her nerve endings until she shivered. She had no idea what he was doing here, but she couldn't look at him without hearing his final words. She couldn't look at him without hearing his rejection, his insistence that he'd never love someone he couldn't trust. "You shouldn't have come."

He scanned her face, his eyes looking for something, and she had no idea what, but self-consciousness made her want to pull away from him, to shut the door. Tears filled her eyes, but she tilted her chin defiantly, needing him to see that she was strong, unbroken, even when she felt the opposite. "You saw your father."

It was the last thing she'd expected him to say. That day felt so long ago now. But his words drew it back to the present, so she felt the whirlwind of pain like it was happening all over again. "What?" She lifted a hand to push her hair back, belatedly remembering she hadn't showered in days, hating the thought of what she must look like.

"That morning. You'd been to see him?"

Her stomach squeezed in a way that was almost unbearable. "So?"

"And you wanted to talk to me about it. You needed me to be there for you and instead…I attacked you." His throat moved as he swallowed.

She looked away, his words hurting when she thought she couldn't hurt any more. "It doesn't matter."

"It matters." He took a step toward her, and she stiffened. He got the message, staying exactly where he was. But his voice softened, and it was almost as though he were touching her. "I meant what I said that day. For six years, I've pushed people away, not trusting anyone, and then I met you and it was like the floodgates were thrown wide open. I let myself feel something I hadn't felt in a really long time. I was blindsided when Jacob told me who you were. Or weren't."

Shame rushed through Ally. "I'm sorry you had to find out that way. I know you have no reason to believe me, but I *was* going to tell you, Luke. I knew I had to and, more than that, I *wanted* to. But I was terrified it would ruin things…"

He jerked his head in agreement. "You were learning to trust as well, and instead of showing you that I was worthy of that, I gave you every reason to think I wasn't," he said quietly, his deep voice rumbling around her porch and into her chest.

Fresh tears filled her throat.

"I was so angry. I was terrified of how I was feeling and what it would mean. I was terrified of the fact you were leaving town, and I didn't know how to make you stay, and more than that, I was terrified that feeling something for you somehow meant I felt less for Jen. When Jacob told me about your name, it gave me a way out. It gave me a way to step away from you and this, to keep things simple, to go back to the way it was before."

She turned her face away, no longer able to look at him.

"I can never go back to that."

She tried to breathe normally.

"I lied to you as well, Ally." He closed the distance now, bringing his body closer to hers. "I lied to you when I said we'd keep it casual. I lied to you when I said it wasn't serious between us. I lied to you when I said I don't trust you and I don't love to you. I lied to you, and I've come here today because you need to at least know the truth."

A silent sob filled her mouth. "Maybe you were right," she whispered, her voice raw. "Maybe we don't love each other. Love shouldn't hurt like this."

"Loving each other isn't what hurts," he said, taking one last step so their bodies were close. "Losing each other is." He lifted his hands then, cupping her face and holding her so they were staring directly at each other. "Walking away from each other, that's what's killing me." He dropped his head forward, pressing their foreheads together. "Having you think I don't love you—I can't accept that. I need you to at least understand that I was wrong to say that. That nothing I said that day is how I feel or what I want."

She pulled backward, moving into the house, and he followed her, closing the door at his back. "You'll never be able to forgive me."

"I already have," he said, and then pulled her into his arms again. "Do you know what it means to trust someone? To have faith in them?"

She didn't say anything.

"It's a gut feeling, an instinct, and it's something you do without any reason sometimes. I trust you. I know you would've told me the truth when you could. I know you didn't come into my life intending to lie to me." He stroked her back, holding her tight, and it felt so good to be in his arms that she didn't fight this, she didn't struggle. She couldn't. She let herself enjoy the closeness, just for a moment. "You gave me a fake name when you had no idea who I was. You gave me a fake name, but you showed me the real you. All of you, including your beautiful, kind heart. The heart that taught me to cook, and helped my daughter to see…"

A small cry came from her lips.

"And I'm the one who owes you an apology. I fought you because of a name, when the essence of who you are is right here inside me. You gave me all of yourself, including your beautiful, precious heart, and I acted like that didn't matter. You needed me to be your friend, to be on your side, and instead I pushed you away. I acted like a fool. I *was* a fool. But if you give me a chance, I'll fix this, Ally. I'll make this right between us again."

She stared up at him, and his words were so exactly what she'd needed to hear for so long that she began to tremble all over. "I lied to you," she whispered.

"You were going to tell me the truth."

Her heart soared, because she had been going to do that. And she knew it to be the truth, and she could feel he could, too.

"We were both caught unawares by this," he said simply. "You didn't set out to lie to me. You didn't set out to lie to Stella. And I think if Jacob hadn't told me, you would have."

"I would have. That day. I was coming to you. I just needed to…breathe." She shook her head, her eyes doleful when they linked with his. "I was so torn. I wanted to run away from Cape Hope, but you were an anchor. Without me realizing it, you and Stella had become a reason for me to stay, and I knew I had to speak to you, to see if you felt…if you were…" She blinked rapidly. "I don't know."

"I'm sorry your dad ever made you feel like you weren't worthy of his love." Luke pulled her tighter. "And I'm more sorry than you could ever know that I did the same thing. If you only knew how much I love you, how much you mean to me…"

She felt the strength of his emotions and her heart exploded. "A part of me died with Jen, and you brought me back to life, Ally. Every sweet, perfect inch of you. Every smile and every laugh, every touch, everything. I never thought I'd fall in love again—but you're all I can think about, all I want, and I just need you to know that. To know that you're a part of my family, and my life, and if I haven't completely screwed everything up, that I want to make this work for us."

A single tear slid down her cheek.

He caught it with his thumb and cradled her face in his palm. "Day follows night, summer follows winter, and happiness comes after grief, Ally. We both deserve happiness."

She sobbed again, but he smiled softly in response, because he clearly understood it wasn't just grief making her body shake.

"I love you," he added gently. "Please come home with me. For Christmas, and forever."

Home.

She turned her head to look around this house of hers, where she'd lived for years, and she felt herself pulling away from it, disconnecting from the physical building, the streets, the landmarks. Because, as much as they were a part of her, they were no longer her world.

Luke and Stella were, and always would be.

"Please say something."

And she laughed, because he'd just poured his heart out, and she'd been unable to get anything out in response.

She tilted her head, her lips parted, waiting for him to kiss her. But he didn't. Instead, he crouched down on one knee, looking up at her, his eyes locked to hers. "I don't have a ring, Ally Monroe, but I have a dream for us and our future. I see a life filled with happiness and love; warmth; big, loud family Christmases; a sister or brother for Stella; and a future so bright we'll need to wear sunglasses all the time—but we're going to reach for it anyway. I want nothing more than to be your future, your everything, forever. Will you marry me?"

Her eyes shone as she nodded, and there wasn't a hint of doubt in her mind. She did love him, and she needed him just as much as he needed her, and she wanted to spend the rest of her life with him and Stella. She chose, in that moment, to believe in happiness and heart, and she knew they'd live happily ever after.

IT WAS IN the early hours of Christmas day when their plane touched down in Cape Hope. They'd talked the whole way, as the plane carried them high above the snow-filled landscape, and they'd laughed, and the certainty that had started in Ally's chest was now in every cell of her body—this was the right decision.

With every minute that passed, she'd felt a tug to Cape Hope and her new life. Whereas the drive to Madison had filled her with a sinking feeling she was traveling in the wrong direction, the return journey filled her with lightheartedness and a sense of sheer, giddy relief.

She was truly going home.

Jacob was still up when the cab pulled into Luke's house.

Luke opened the door to the house and put an arm around Ally's shoulders, keeping her hugged close to his chest. He'd called Jacob before they boarded their flight. She didn't know what was said, but Luke had reassured Ally that all would be well.

Still, she fretted, with no idea how Jen's brother, the no-nonsense town cop, would take her return—nor if he'd ever accept her place in Luke and Stella's life.

Jacob stood when they walked in, an almost sheepish expression on his face. "Hey." He held a hand out to Luke. "Merry Christmas."

"Merry Christmas." Luke grinned, squeezing Ally tighter.

"Jacob, I'd like you to meet my fiancée, Ally Monroe."

Ally's own smile was a little sheepish. "Not Amy."

"I gathered." Jacob nodded, but there was a smile on his face, as though he wanted to smooth over her small lie. Her heart swelled, because, of course, he did—he loved Luke and Stella, and so did she. How could they not make their peace? "It's nice to meet you, Ally. Welcome to the family." And he opened his arms wide, drawing her into a big bear hug.

Ridiculously, tears of happiness sparkled on Ally's lashes.

Later, when Jacob had disappeared into the guest room and Ally and Luke were sitting up drinking her famous eggnog, he asked her about her emotional response.

"I just came here with no family, feeling so completely alone, and now I have all of you. I feel…very blessed."

Luke reached across and put his hand on hers, his eyes crinkled at the corners as he smiled at his fiancée. "There's no one on earth who deserves that more than you."

CHRISTMAS MORNING STARTED with a squeal. "Oh my goodness!"

Ally winced, flipping the pancake before turning around to see Stella staring up at her with wide eyes.

"You're home!"

Ally's heart twisted at how right this felt. "Uh-huh."

"For how long?"

Luke appeared behind Stella, a brow quirked. Ally swallowed and nodded at Luke.

"Honey, we were thinking she might stay. Forever. What do you think?"

Stella looked from one to the other. "Really?"

Ally froze, needing Stella's approval before she could really relax and celebrate this new life of theirs.

"Really," Luke said. "What do you think?"

"I think it's the best Christmas ever!" She ran to Ally and flung her arms around her waist. "You were my Christmas wish, and you came true!"

Ally thought then of the shooting star, and how she'd held a secret wish deep in her heart as it had sailed across the sky.

She crouched down and wrapped her arms around Stella, holding her tight. "Mine, too."

DAY FOLLOWED NIGHT, and summer followed winter, and, by the following summer, Ally's tummy was round with new life, new hope. A little brother for Stella, and a new son for the town of Cape Hope.

And every morning, as she sat down to breakfast with Stella and Luke, the knowledge that they'd soon have another little person at their table, she knew how right she'd been to choose hope over fear and love over loneliness. She'd opened herself up to family, and she'd found herself right where she belonged.

But it wasn't just her place in the Miller family that had been carved out.

A month after coming to live with Luke and Stella, a bundle of forwarded mail had arrived from Wisconsin and, in it, familiar handwriting on one envelope.

With shaking fingers, she'd opened the back and begun to read it aloud, to herself and Luke:

My dear Alicia,

I thought living without my daughter in my life was hard before, but now that I've seen you again, it is a daily agony. I was wrong twenty years ago. Wrong eighteen years ago, sixteen years ago. I have been wrong every day that I didn't go to you and explain. I can't change the past, but I can tell you now how much I would wish to, if I could.

I love you.

You're my daughter and I want you to be a part of my life when you're ready. I'm not going anywhere. I want to know you, and I hope, one day, you decide you want to know me.

Please know how sorry I am, how wrong I was.

Love,
Dad.

She'd read it every day for a week before Luke, with

whom she'd shared the letter as soon as she'd received it, brought it up once more.

"I'll come with you," he'd offered.

At first, she'd shaken her head. She hadn't been ready.

But as days had turned into weeks and the letter had sat inside her heart, she'd felt a pull to her dad that wouldn't go away.

A month after it had arrived, with Luke at her side, they'd walked into Cup of Joe.

It had started slowly. Coffee in the café, a few conversations, but gradually the relationship had built, and now they had dinner together regularly. It would never be the relationship Ally might have wanted; she'd probably never forgive her dad with all of her heart, but she could still love him. She could still make room for him in their lives.

So she did—and she was happier for it.

By the time their son arrived, the leaves were beginning to fall from the trees and it was cold again. Ally held baby Wade in her arms and smiled, because winters would come and winters would go, but it would always be warm again.

There was always warmth in her life now, and she knew there always would be.

The End

If you enjoyed this book, please leave a review at your favorite online retailer! Even if it's just a sentence or two it makes all the difference.

Thanks for reading *Christmas with the Firefighter* by Clare Connelly!

Discover your next romance at TulePublishing.com.

TULE

PUBLISHING

If you enjoyed *Christmas with the Firefighter*,
you'll love these other Tule Christmas books!

Sleigh Bell Farms
by Kaylie Newell

The Christmas Contest
by Scarlet Wilson

The Christmas Pony
by Nancy Holland

Available now at your favorite online retailer!

About the Author

Clare Connelly writes romance that will set your soul on fire. She is the best-selling author of more than seventy romance novels. She reads and writes romance voraciously, and lives in a small bungalow by the sea with her lovely husband, two small children and a hard-working team of MacBooks.

Visit her website at www.clareconnelly.com.

Thank you for reading

Christmas with the Firefighter

If you enjoyed this book, you can find more from all our great authors at TulePublishing.com, or from your favorite online retailer.

TULE
PUBLISHING

Lightning Source UK Ltd.
Milton Keynes UK
UKHW012237131220
375115UK00001B/123

9 781951 190187